# AXEL

LANTERN BEACH BLACKOUT: THE NEW RECRUITS, BOOK 2

CHRISTY BARRITT

Copyright © 2021 by Christy Barritt

All rights reserved.

No part of this book may be reproduced in any form or by any electronic or mechanical means, including information storage and retrieval systems, without written permission from the author, except for the use of brief quotations in a book review.

COMPLETE BOOK LIST

**Squeaky Clean Mysteries:**
- #1 Hazardous Duty
- #2 Suspicious Minds
- #2.5 It Came Upon a Midnight Crime (novella)
- #3 Organized Grime
- #4 Dirty Deeds
- #5 The Scum of All Fears
- #6 To Love, Honor and Perish
- #7 Mucky Streak
- #8 Foul Play
- #9 Broom & Gloom
- #10 Dust and Obey
- #11 Thrill Squeaker
- #11.5 Swept Away (novella)
- #12 Cunning Attractions
- #13 Cold Case: Clean Getaway

#14 Cold Case: Clean Sweep
#15 Cold Case: Clean Break
#16 Cleans to an End
While You Were Sweeping, A Riley Thomas Spinoff

**The Sierra Files:**
#1 Pounced
#2 Hunted
#3 Pranced
#4 Rattled

**The Gabby St. Claire Diaries (a Tween Mystery series):**
The Curtain Call Caper
The Disappearing Dog Dilemma
The Bungled Bike Burglaries

**The Worst Detective Ever**
#1 Ready to Fumble
#2 Reign of Error
#3 Safety in Blunders
#4 Join the Flub
#5 Blooper Freak
#6 Flaw Abiding Citizen
#7 Gaffe Out Loud
#8 Joke and Dagger
#9 Wreck the Halls

#10 Glitch and Famous

**Raven Remington**
Relentless 1
Relentless 2 (coming soon)

**Holly Anna Paladin Mysteries:**
#1 Random Acts of Murder
#2 Random Acts of Deceit
#2.5 Random Acts of Scrooge
#3 Random Acts of Malice
#4 Random Acts of Greed
#5 Random Acts of Fraud
#6 Random Acts of Outrage
#7 Random Acts of Iniquity

**Lantern Beach Mysteries**
#1 Hidden Currents
#2 Flood Watch
#3 Storm Surge
#4 Dangerous Waters
#5 Perilous Riptide
#6 Deadly Undertow

**Lantern Beach Romantic Suspense**
Tides of Deception
Shadow of Intrigue
Storm of Doubt

Winds of Danger
Rains of Remorse
Torrents of Fear

**Lantern Beach P.D.**
On the Lookout
Attempt to Locate
First Degree Murder
Dead on Arrival
Plan of Action

**Lantern Beach Escape**
Afterglow (a novelette)

**Lantern Beach Blackout**
Dark Water
Safe Harbor
Ripple Effect
Rising Tide

**Lantern Beach Guardians**
Hide and Seek
Shock and Awe
Safe and Sound

**Lantern Beach Blackout: The New Recruits**
Rocco

**Crime á la Mode**
Deadman's Float
Milkshake Up
Bomb Pop Threat
Banana Split Personalities

**The Sidekick's Survival Guide**
The Art of Eavesdropping
The Perks of Meddling
The Exercise of Interfering
The Practice of Prying
The Skill of Snooping
The Craft of Being Covert

**Saltwater Cowboys**
Saltwater Cowboy
Breakwater Protector
Cape Corral Keeper
Seagrass Secrets
Driftwood Danger

**Carolina Moon Series**
Home Before Dark
Gone By Dark
Wait Until Dark
Light the Dark
Taken By Dark

**Suburban Sleuth Mysteries:**
　　Death of the Couch Potato's Wife

**Fog Lake Suspense:**
　　Edge of Peril
　　Margin of Error
　　Brink of Danger
　　Line of Duty

**Cape Thomas Series:**
　　Dubiosity
　　Disillusioned
　　Distorted

**Standalone Romantic Mystery:**
　　The Good Girl

**Suspense:**
　　Imperfect
　　The Wrecking

**Sweet Christmas Novella:**
　　Home to Chestnut Grove

**Standalone Romantic-Suspense:**
　　Keeping Guard
　　The Last Target
　　Race Against Time

Ricochet

Key Witness

Lifeline

High-Stakes Holiday Reunion

Desperate Measures

Hidden Agenda

Mountain Hideaway

Dark Harbor

Shadow of Suspicion

The Baby Assignment

The Cradle Conspiracy

Trained to Defend

Mountain Survival

**Nonfiction:**

Characters in the Kitchen

Changed: True Stories of Finding God through Christian Music (out of print)

The Novel in Me: The Beginner's Guide to Writing and Publishing a Novel (out of print)

# CHAPTER ONE

OLIVIA ROLLINS nearly jumped out of her skin as something crashed.

She froze and jerked her gaze toward the front of The Crazy Chefette.

A plate.

Someone had just dropped a dirty plate and it clattered unbroken on the floor.

She let out a chuckle, releasing a burst of air from her lungs as she did so.

It was no big deal. Another waitress had already started to clean the mess up and didn't appear to need any help.

Olivia willed her heart to slow its frantic pace.

*You're safe here. You can breathe. You can live again.*

But her personal pep talk didn't help. Her muscles were still pulled taut.

When would she stop feeling so jumpy?

Probably never.

Especially when she remembered the note she'd found outside her apartment this morning.

*My love, you're so beautiful. I can't wait until we meet.*

It sounded innocent, she supposed.

But she had no idea who had left it.

The one person she could think of shouldn't know she was in Lantern Beach.

But what if he did?

She shuddered at the thought and started cleaning off the recently vacated table.

Yet Olivia couldn't stop looking around, searching for any signs of trouble.

Survival instinct had programmed her to keep her eyes wide open. Always.

As she scanned the dining area of the restaurant again, her gaze stopped on a man across the room.

Instead of feeling fear, annoyance flashed through her.

The man was handsome with his arrogant smile, rebellious gaze, and devil-may-care attitude. He was tall and lean with smooth but sculpted muscles. His dark brown hair was slightly messy. He looked like he hadn't shaved this morning. Then again, he always looked like that.

It wasn't the man's presence that bothered her. No, it was the women—mostly college-aged tourists

—who drooled all over him and the fact that Olivia had to daily witness it like a bad replay of *Groundhog Day*.

She continued wiping the table, only glancing up long enough to roll her eyes at the three women surrounding this guy now.

"You've got to be kidding me," she muttered beneath her breath.

The bathing-suit-clad ladies giggled at something he said, and the man's eyes sparkled as he entertained them like some kind of edgy, model-worthy Casanova.

It was like he was a magnet, and they were spiky shards of metal that gravitated toward him at a terrifying force.

Olivia knew his type, and she didn't like men like him.

No, next time she dated—*if* she ever dated again—she wanted a man who was boring. Who didn't attract attention. Who preferred a desk to a gym.

In other words, the total opposite of that guy.

She heard someone say he was a Navy SEAL.

Olivia would bet he'd made that up just to impress the ladies. Some guys did that.

"He's a real cutie, huh?"

Olivia looked up as her boss, Lisa Dillinger, approached from the kitchen. The woman—in her late twenties—had braided her blonde hair, and it fell over one shoulder. Her wholesome smile seemed to make her glow, no matter how crazy or stressful it got inside the restaurant during the summer rush.

Then Olivia remembered Lisa's statement and scoffed. "A real cutie? That's not *exactly* what I was thinking. He's *precisely* the kind of guy I stay away from."

Lisa followed her gaze and smiled, shifting a black tub of empty cups to her other hip. "Axel's not all that bad. He's actually pretty nice."

Axel? The name seemed fitting for the motorcycle-loving ladies' man.

Olivia raised her eyebrows. "You know the man?"

Lisa grabbed an empty cup from another table and nodded. "As a matter of fact, Braden is friends with him."

Braden was Lisa's husband. The man, a police officer on the island, seemed like an all-around good guy. Certainly, Lisa and Braden were good judges of character, right?

It didn't matter. Olivia wouldn't be falling under this guy's spell any time soon. Or ever, for that matter.

Olivia rose to full height—five eight, just tall enough to feel like an Amazon warrior in high school —and picked up her spray bottle, satisfied that the table had been properly sanitized.

"Just don't make me wait on him. Please."

Lisa smiled again and continued to collect some used plates. "You're so funny. But you've been a big help to me since you started working here, so if you don't want to wait his table then, by all means, don't wait his table."

"Sounds good. I'd hate to accidentally spill a drink on him or something."

"You wouldn't . . ."

"I'd blame it on his startling good looks . . ." Olivia laughed.

Lisa moaned. "Just do me a favor after you deliver your next order. Take the trash out for me."

"You got it." Olivia stepped toward the kitchen as she heard a bell clang. Time to see if the family of five two tables over could finally eat their dinner.

Olivia delivered food to the family and refilled their drinks. Then she went to run the trash out to the dumpster. The can was getting full and would start smelling soon.

Working at a small establishment like this, employees did a little bit of everything. Waitressing. Hosting. Busing tables.

She grabbed the trash and twisted the top of the bag together. Heaving the bag over her shoulder, Olivia opened the back door and stepped into the nighttime. The air was heavy with humidity from the ninety-degree heat earlier in the day. Even being two blocks from the ocean, she still caught a whiff of the salty air.

Something about it always calmed her.

Before moving farther, she glanced around.

Olivia thought that coming here to Lantern Beach she might be able to relax more, to let down her guard. But she couldn't. At least not for an extended period of time. Only for brief seconds, like when she inhaled the scent of the sea.

As she studied her surroundings, she ran her thumb across her ring finger. She half expected to feel the engagement ring there.

But it was gone.

Thank goodness, it was gone.

The jewelry had felt more like a three hundred-pound weight than the promise of happily ever after.

When Olivia confirmed the area behind the restaurant was empty, she hurried across the gravel lot toward the dumpster.

If anyone saw her, they'd think she was crazy for moving so fast.

She'd never been the type to get spooked before.

But Tristan had changed that.

Just the thought of him caused her skin to crawl. How long would he have this hold over her life, over her reactions?

It had already been too long.

Quickly, she threw the trash into the dumpster, let the lid slam closed, and then wiped her hands on her jeans.

Job done.

As she turned to go back inside, she collided with someone.

She looked up, and her throat went dry.

"Tristan..." The word came out as a gasp.

The next instant, his meaty hand gripped her arm, and he shoved her against the dumpster. Her head hit the metal, causing an immediate throb.

"Long time no see," Tristan Bennett muttered as he glared down at her.

Olivia's knees went weak at the sight of him, at the sound of his menacing voice, at the memory of his overpowering strength.

He'd found her.

And no one was here to help her escape.

---

AXEL HENDRIX STRETCHED his arm across the back of the booth and glanced up at the giggling blonde standing beside his table. Her two friends had run to the bathroom. He was pretty sure they'd had some type of silent conversation, and this blonde had been declared the winner—the one left here alone with him.

That meant it was time to end this conversation.

With another shrug, he finished his story with, "And that's how it all went down."

He always liked to wrap things up with that line.

He thought it added flair. Kind of like Paul Harvey saying, "And that's the rest of the story." His granddad had loved listening to those radiocasts, and Axel had happily been entertained with him.

"I think you're amazing." The woman practically purred as she leaned toward Axel. "Just amazing."

Based on the look in her eyes, Axel was the trophy and flirting was her means to win. He pushed away his plate—the one that had contained a bacon cheeseburger and fries—and glanced at his watch.

It was time to go. He had other things to do.

Besides, Axel didn't want to lead this woman on.

She was pretty enough. But he recognized that look in her eyes.

The challenge.

The aggressive ones always seemed to find him and consider him as a conquest.

None of the women he'd met since coming here to Lantern Beach wanted to get to know *him*. Maybe they were fascinated with bad boys, and they thought he was one because of his motorcycle. Or maybe they'd heard he'd been a Navy SEAL, and they were fascinated with the person they thought he should be.

But Axel had been around long enough to know he wanted someone who didn't care about either of those things.

Besides, he had other issues to worry about.

Especially since women were going missing up and down the East Coast.

He wished he was in here tonight just to have fun, but he wasn't. He was here to watch. To observe. To protect.

If the intel they'd received was correct, the next victim would be snatched from this area.

He smiled at the blonde, ready to wrap up this conversation. "Well, it was really great to meet you . . . Brenda."

"Pamela." She batted her eyelashes, not looking the least bit bothered by his slipup.

He stood. "Sorry about that, *Pamela*."

She stepped back . . . but only slightly. Axel had to back away in order not to press up against her as he slipped past.

"Maybe I'll see you again sometime while I'm in town." She touched his arm and winked before sauntering back a step.

"You never know." He dropped a twenty on the table before pretending to see somebody outside and waving. "Sorry. I've got to run now."

Before Pamela could keep the conversation going, Axel headed toward the door. These superficial interactions were easy—much easier than diving into a deep relationship. Besides, ever since Mandy, he'd had no desire to put his heart on the line again.

Women thought they wanted to date men in his

line of work. But they didn't—not when they discovered the nitty-gritty details about his job. About the days away from home. About the nightmares that came from the battles he'd waged. About the times when his job—and the things he'd seen—remained tethered to him like a ball and chain.

Quickly, Axel stepped outside into the thick, humid beach air and took a deep breath.

On the outside, he was a master at conversations like the ones he'd had inside. The flirting games, so to speak. But on the inside, he felt as if he couldn't breathe.

He turned the corner of the building, heading to where he'd left his motorcycle. He needed to get back to the Blackout facility. An impromptu meeting had been scheduled this evening. Maybe someone had an update on their latest assignment.

Several hotel chains were linked in the disappearance of six women in the past four months. The one thing that connected the disappearances and hotel chains?

Oasis Management Systems had developed each hotel's booking and check-in system.

That company's executives just happened to be on Lantern Beach this week for a corporate retreat.

Just as he was about to slip his helmet on, a sound caught his ear.

Had that been a cry?

He paused, wondering what he'd heard. A cat maybe.

The same noise filled the air again.

That was *definitely* a cry. A *human* cry.

He dropped his helmet and darted toward the noise.

As he rounded the corner, he spotted the pretty waitress from the restaurant. The one with sun-kissed brown hair to her shoulders. A slim build. A fire in her gaze.

Of course, he'd noticed her when he'd been inside. What hot-blooded male wouldn't?

A tall, broad man cornered her against the dumpster, his fist poised in the air as if he were about to strike.

She slid to the ground, arms up in a defensive gesture.

Axel's muscles tightened.

He wasn't going to let this happen.

# CHAPTER TWO

OLIVIA DREW her knees to her chest, trying to protect herself from the oncoming pain.

She'd seen Tristan mad before . . . but never like this.

Today, she felt his threats might actually be true.

A gasp caught in her throat at the thought of it.

"Get away from her!" a deep voice yelled.

The next instant, Tristan jerked back.

Olivia's eyes widened when she spotted the bristled man behind Tristan.

Axel.

She held her breath as she waited for whatever would play out next.

It was noble of Mr. Casanova to try to help her. But Tristan . . . he was a beast. Not someone to be messed with. Especially not by a womanizing biker who probably slid by on his good looks.

The man wouldn't stand a chance against Tristan.

"You should stay out of this," Tristan growled. He turned toward the man, his muscles taut, his jaw hard, and his fists ready for action.

Olivia held her breath.

She knew what was coming.

But she was powerless to stop the rage-fueled beating about to happen.

Axel stepped closer, defiance filling his gaze. If he felt any fear, he didn't show it. "I said, get away from her."

Tristan let out a warning growl before swinging his fist at the man.

"No!" Olivia yelled.

Tristan would beat this man until he was unrecognizable. He wouldn't stop until his opponent lay in a crumpled heap, hovering on the edge of death.

Before Tristan's fist met his jaw, Axel ducked. His elbow plowed Tristan's abdomen.

Her ex doubled over and stumbled back.

Olivia scrambled away, not wanting the Goliath-like man to crush her. But Tristan righted himself and drew in several deep, furious breaths.

As footsteps sounded in the distance, Tristan paused. His posture remained hulking, almost as if he might lose it and go all barbarian on Axel.

Then Tristan seemed to realize the situation he'd put himself in the middle of.

He glared at Olivia again before stepping back. Testosterone surrounded him like pollution formed a haze around a city.

"This isn't over," he snarled.

The next moment, he dashed toward the road.

Axel watched him leave then knelt in front of Olivia. "Are you okay?"

He sounded so sincere that Olivia wondered if he was a different person for a moment. Guys like him weren't supposed to have sweet sides—unless they wanted to use them to their advantage. That was most likely the case here. She needed to keep that in mind.

Olivia nodded, even though her trembles told the real truth.

She was terrified.

How had Tristan found her?

Had he followed her here to Lantern Beach?

Olivia had made it clear to the man when she'd ended things that they had no future together. But Tristan wasn't the type of guy who took no for an answer. Olivia had known that, but she'd hoped for the best. Hoped for the best but prepared for the worst.

"How about we get you inside?" Axel extended his hand.

After a moment of hesitation, Olivia slipped her fingers into his.

She ignored the charge that zapped through her blood as their skin touched. That was just her pain talking. Nothing more.

Axel helped Olivia to her feet, and she quickly released her hand from his.

As she did, Lisa dashed to Olivia's side. "Olivia . . . what happened? I stepped out and . . . did that guy hit you?"

Olivia shook her head, hating the negative attention. All she'd wanted was to disappear, to not be seen. She thought waitressing would be an easy job until she figured out her future. She'd thought she could remain unattached to anyone in this area.

Yet here she was.

"No . . . he didn't hit me. Not really." Olivia's voice cracked. "He just got a little rough."

Axel's gaze darkened. "Do you want to press charges? I can go after him and—"

"No, please. I just want to forget that ever happened," she rushed. "All of this is embarrassing, to be honest."

The fact someone treated Olivia so poorly showed a weak side to herself she'd rather keep hidden. She'd been successful in her career, independent in her lifestyle, and had graduated at the top of her class.

Yet one person had reduced her to a quivering mess.

She hated herself for letting that happen. She always thought she'd be stronger than that.

But she wasn't.

"You have nothing to be embarrassed about." Axel's voice sounded calm and reassuring. But it hardened as his gaze followed the trail where Tristan had disappeared. "But that guy does."

Olivia opened her mouth, trying to find a response. But she had nothing. Only exhaustion. Fear. Relief.

She wobbled at the thought of what had just happened.

And what might have happened.

Axel took her elbow, helping to hold her steady. "Let's get inside. I want to make sure you're okay."

Thankfully, Olivia *was* okay. This time, at least.

And it was all thanks to the very man she thought she despised ... Mr. Casanova.

---

FURY BURNED inside Axel as he paced in front of Olivia. She sat at a chair in the kitchen of the restaurant, holding a bag of ice to the back of her head where a knot had formed.

If there was one thing he hated, it was seeing men treat women like that guy had treated Olivia.

If Axel hadn't gotten there when he had . . . this might be a different story.

Was Olivia really trying to protect that coward who'd manhandled her? He knew abuse could be complicated. That the psychology behind it wasn't always simple. But still . . . there was no excuse for what that guy had done.

Axel paused with his hands on his hips. Despite his outrage, he knew he needed to soften his tone. He didn't want to frighten Olivia any more than she already was.

"Who was that guy?" he asked.

"He's my ex-boyfriend." With her free hand, Olivia grabbed a tissue and ran it beneath her eyes as mascara flooded down her cheeks. "I'm sorry. I don't mean to react like this. I just didn't expect to see him here."

"Olivia, it's okay." Lisa knelt in front of her, the picture of a calm and nurturing friend—just as Lisa was known to be.

"Did you tell this guy you were coming here?" Axel continued, trying to get a better understanding of the situation—even if it wasn't any of his business.

"No. I don't know how he found me."

Axel's jaw tightened. "Do you have a restraining order against him?"

Olivia shook her head. "No, I decided to come here and start fresh instead of going through all that back home. I just thought . . . I just thought moving was the better option. But I didn't mean to bring trouble with me or to involve any of you. I'm sorry."

"Don't apologize." Axel rubbed his neck. "This wasn't your fault."

She wiped under her eyes one more time before placing her ice pack on the table, drawing in a deep breath, and standing. "I should get back to work."

Lisa frowned. "Why don't you take some time? I can handle things here."

Olivia waved her hand in the air. "I'll be fine. Really. Let me work. It will distract me."

But as Axel watched her walk away, he seriously doubted that.

That man—Tristan, she'd said his name was—had known exactly how to find Olivia.

He would be back.

Axel had no doubt about that.

He wasn't sure what it was about the woman that made his protective instincts rise. Then again, he'd feel this way about any woman, really.

Axel's dad had been a vile man who'd liked to use his fists on Axel's mother.

Harming a woman was never okay. Never.

He crossed his arms as he watched Olivia quickly wash her hands before disappearing back into the dining area.

Pretending this never happened wasn't going to

work. But how could Axel possibly help if Olivia didn't want him to step in?

As he glanced at Lisa, Axel sensed that her thoughts mirrored his own.

The town's newest waitress needed their help.

But would she accept it?

## CHAPTER THREE

OLIVIA COUNTED down the minutes until she finished her shift. Although only two people—plus Tristan—were aware of what happened behind the restaurant, every time someone glanced at her, she felt like they knew.

Paranoia twisted her thoughts, her reality.

The past three months had been blissful without Tristan. For a while, Olivia actually thought she'd managed to break away from the stronghold he held on her life.

But, apparently, she was wrong.

How could someone who'd succeeded in so many areas fall apart so easily at the hands of another person? It didn't make sense.

The truth was Olivia had no choice but to leave her job as a marketing consultant back in Kentucky.

Coming to this isolated island and working a job as a waitress felt like the reset button she'd been longing for.

But maybe she'd been wrong.

Finally, her shift ended. As she stood by the restaurant's back door and looked out the window at the dark parking lot, a tremble raked through her.

What if Tristan waited out there for her? Olivia might not be so lucky when he confronted her the next time. What if she didn't have Mr. Casanova waiting there to save the day?

She flushed every time she thought about Axel stepping in. He might be smaller than Tristan, but he had a warrior's spirit that was equal, if not bigger, in size. He hadn't shown even a hint of fear as he'd gone up against Goliath.

Then there was Tristan, who was all muscle—muscle born of protein shakes and obsessive workouts. His reactions were fueled by anger and possessiveness. His motives were purely selfish—always.

"Listen, why don't you wait until Braden gets here?" Lisa paused beside her, a bag of flour in her arms. "He can walk you out. He's due back any minute now."

"I'll be fine. Tristan won't be back tonight." Olivia wished she felt as certain as she sounded.

"Then let me walk you out." Lisa put the bag on the counter, wiped her hands, and stepped toward the door.

Olivia shook her head. Lisa had a small child—a ten-month-old girl named Julia. The last thing Olivia wanted was to put her boss in danger. And Tristan . . . well, Olivia wouldn't put anything past him.

"Really, I'll be fine. My car is parked on the side of the building, and I have my mace just in case I need it." Olivia fished the spray canister from her pocket and held it up.

Lisa stared at her another moment, doubt lingering in her gaze. "I really want to walk you out. I'd feel much better if I did."

Olivia frowned, knowing how stubborn Lisa could be. "How about if you watch me from the door instead? If you see trouble, you can call the police."

Lisa frowned but finally said, "I suppose that would work."

After thanking Lisa and telling her good night, Olivia opened the back door and stepped outside.

She paused a moment as the sound of crickets surrounded her.

Just crickets.

No unseen footsteps. No hidden figures.

She stepped farther from the safety of the door, willing herself not to run all the way to her vehicle.

But as soon as her feet hit the gravel lot, a voice filled the air.

"I was hoping I might run into you again."

Olivia froze as fear overtook her.

AXEL FROWNED when he saw the terror on Olivia's face.

He started to explain when Olivia raised her hand.

Axel's eyes widened when saw the mace there.

He ducked just as she pressed the button on the canister and sprayed it at him.

As the fumes filled the air, Axel coughed and scowled. That had been close. He'd avoided a direct hit, but this stuff was still potent.

"What are you doing?" His voice climbed in pitch as he stepped away.

She stood there a moment, looking dumbfounded as she continued to hold the canister, looking poised to use it again. "You . . . scared me. I . . . just reacted."

He straightened, keeping one eye on the mace and waving the residuals away from his face. "You can put that away. Please."

She nodded, still looking like she was in shock as she put the canister into her pocket. "Sorry."

He coughed again before murmuring, "It's okay."

"What are you doing out here?" Olivia rolled her shoulders as if trying to pull herself together.

He hadn't tried to hide his presence. In fact, he'd been sitting in plain sight on his motorcycle, knowing that The Crazy Chefette had just closed and that the pretty waitress would be leaving soon.

He would have gone in to tell her he was waiting outside, on the lookout for any signs of trouble. But he had a feeling the act of chivalry wouldn't be welcome.

Apparently, his Plan B hadn't been a good idea either.

He rubbed his neck. "I just wanted to make sure that trouble didn't show up again. I didn't mean to scare you."

Lisa stuck her head out the door. "Everything okay?"

"We're fine," Olivia called. "Just a little misunderstanding."

Lisa frowned before nodding and waving again. She slipped back inside, but Axel saw her lingering in the doorway still as if double-checking that Olivia's words were true.

Olivia turned back to him and said nothing for a moment before snapping back into action. She hurried past him toward her car, an icy bristliness to her steps.

"That was nice of you to wait for me," she murmured. "But I'm fine."

Clearly, she wasn't fine.

"I don't like what happened earlier," Axel stated.

She paused and turned toward him, something flashing in her gaze. Anger? Irritation? Prideful stubbornness? He wasn't sure.

"Listen," she started. "I know you have good intentions. But I didn't ask for your help."

Axel ignored her sharp words. "What does that guy want with you?"

Defiance flashed in her gaze. Olivia didn't think it was any of Axel's business. And it wasn't.

But that wouldn't stop him from asking.

"I don't know." She shrugged. "He wants what he wants, and he usually gets it. Isn't that enough?"

Axel continued to stare at her. "What's his last name?"

She shifted by her car door, not bothering to hide her mounting irritation. "Really?"

"I want to figure out where he's staying."

"I'm going to have to repeat what I just said. I appreciate your concern. But I'll handle this on my own."

"Is that what you call what you did earlier? Handling it?"

Olivia's hands fisted at her side. But Axel knew she couldn't argue with his assessment. The man had been about to strike, and Olivia had been on the ground at that guy's mercy.

"I've got to get home," she muttered, turning back to her car.

Maybe Axel's approach hadn't been the best—though he'd tried. He really had.

But he wanted to talk this through with her more.

He softened his tone as he said, "I'm sorry. I don't mean to sound bossy. I know you don't know me."

Olivia fumbled with her keys, not bothering to look back and make eye contact. "That's right, I don't know you. But I know your type."

Axel stepped back and crossed his arms at her frosty tone. "My type?"

She turned toward him, her gaze fiery. "Yes, your type. The one who wants to be the big man on campus. The hero who swoops in to save the day. The guy every woman wants to be with." She shook her head and opened her car door. "I'm sorry. But I'm not like those other women. And I don't want to owe anyone anything."

Before Axel could say anything else, Olivia climbed into her car and slammed the door. She offered one more glance at him as she pulled away.

Axel watched her leave.

That hadn't gone the way he planned.

He should probably just ignore his instinct to help.

But another part of him knew that would be nearly impossible.

Because he could practically smell the danger in the air.

## CHAPTER FOUR

OLIVIA STEPPED INTO HER APARTMENT, hardly able to breathe.

She'd like to think of this place as her safe space, but she hadn't lived here long enough to say that. Besides, her upstairs neighbor blared music at all times of the night, and she was pretty sure her neighbor downstairs smoked weed.

Lantern Beach might be a popular vacation spot, but this complex was one of the few areas of affordable housing on the island for minimum-wage employees. That meant that some residents—like the ones who came to the area to surf while making some money on the side—often stayed in one of the nine apartments here and lived out their beach life dreams.

It wasn't the most notable of clientele, and it was quite a change from the condo Olivia had owned in

Kentucky. The three-bedroom home had only been minutes from downtown Lexington, and people needed a key card to enter the eight-story building.

She paused inside her front door and glanced around.

The place wasn't large—just a great room with a kitchen, bathroom, and bedroom. The laundry area was shared by residents in an area downstairs.

At least the place had come furnished, even if the upholstery on most of the furniture looked well used.

The good news was that there weren't many places to hide here in the small space.

Everything, based on her quick scan, looked just the same as Olivia had left it when she'd gone into work nine hours ago.

Before she stepped inside farther, a noise cut through the air.

She flinched and reached for the door handle.

Then she realized it was just her cell phone.

She nearly laughed at herself.

As she pulled the device from her pocket and glanced at the screen, any amusement left her. Instead, dread filled her stomach when she saw Tristan's name.

How had he gotten her number? Olivia had changed it when she moved here, and she'd only given her new digits to a few people—people she knew she could trust.

She'd figure out that answer later. Right now, she stared at her phone.

She should ignore the call.

Olivia frowned. No, on second thought, maybe she needed to deal with Tristan head on. Quivering and hiding wouldn't get her anywhere. Besides, she liked to think of herself as a fighter. What had happened to that spunky spirit she was once known for?

She sighed as she hit Talk and put the phone to her ear. "What do you want?"

"Is that any way to greet the man you almost married?"

She froze.

That voice...

She jerked her head up.

It hadn't come from her phone.

She gasped as a figure stepped from the shadows.

---

AXEL CLIMBED on his motorcycle and started down the two-lane road that ran down the center of the long, narrow island.

There was nothing like being on his bike and riding by the ocean, where he could feel the salty breeze coming off the water.

This bike—a Harley Davidson V-Rod—had been his present to himself when he left the military a year ago. He needed something to keep his adventurous side alive.

Then he'd been offered a job with the private security agency Blackout. So maybe he didn't need the motorcycle anymore. But he wasn't giving the bike up.

As he headed down the road toward the Blackout facility, his mind raced. He couldn't stop mentally replaying what had just happened. He was so thankful he'd stepped outside when he had. Otherwise, that woman . . . Olivia . . . she could be seriously hurt right now.

He'd seen it happen one too many times.

Axel had grown up here on this island. For most people, that meant a happy childhood. But not with a father like his.

Most of the time, Axel had simply tried to protect his mom. He'd even gotten socked in the jaw a few times himself during the process.

The only thing that had helped him keep his sanity was heading to the beach to surf. Being out on the waves made him forget all his troubles.

That had always been his MO. He was a risk-taker. An adventure seeker.

That's why becoming a SEAL had been the ideal job for him. He'd been able to serve his country through high-stake operations.

He continued that now through Blackout.

As he headed down the road, he noticed a flash of headlights beside him.

He zipped into the other lane to avoid the car that pulled out from a side street. The driver didn't stop before turning onto the main highway and nearly sideswiped Axel.

He glanced forward.

Another vehicle headed toward him, coming from the opposite direction.

He had to get back into his lane.

Now.

But the car flanking the other side of him wasn't moving fast enough. The vehicle seemed to hover beside him instead, keeping his same pace.

That meant Axel was trapped in the wrong lane with a vehicle approaching him head-on.

He gripped the throttle on his bike as he felt his adrenaline kick in.

He had to make a split-second decision.

Axel tried to motion to the other driver, who clearly hadn't seen him when pulling out onto the highway.

But the dark-tinted windows of the sedan meant he couldn't see the person behind the wheel.

Axel looked in front of him again and saw he only had several feet before the oncoming car hit him. It was too late to lower his speed and try to drop behind the car beside him.

Instead, he jerked to the left, to the side of the road.

As he did, his wheels hit the gravel. His bike veered toward the ditch beside him.

And before he could stop, he careened into the deep crevice.

## CHAPTER FIVE

TRISTAN SMIRKED as he stepped closer, emerging from Olivia's dark bedroom.

"How did you get inside?" Olivia's muscles tensed as she tried to prepare herself for whatever was about to happen.

"That's my little secret." His voice sounded mocking, and his cool tones made it clear he knew he was in control right now. He loved being the one calling the shots.

Olivia moved away and her back hit the wall. Her head throbbed again, a reminder of their earlier confrontation.

She glanced around her, looking for a weapon.

But there was nothing within reach—only a canvas picture on the wall behind her.

"Actually, I'm here for a corporate retreat," Tristan

said. "I happened to see your car at the restaurant when I was going past. I planned on going inside to talk with you. Then you stepped out back, and things turned ugly when your friend came after me like that."

*Axel* was the one who had made things turn ugly?

Disgust rose in her.

"Why are you here now?" Olivia demanded. "This is my apartment. You have no right to be inside without my permission."

"I have a favor to ask of you." Tristan acted as if he hadn't heard her previous statement.

"*You* want to ask *me* for a favor?" Olivia didn't bother to keep the derision from her voice. "Why would I want to do anything to help you?"

His eyes narrowed and he took a step closer. "Because if you do this for me, I'll leave you alone."

Leave her alone? That would be an answer to her prayers. But could she even hope that might be a possibility?

"Why won't you just leave me alone anyway?" she asked.

"And let you off the hook that easily? After what you did to me? You refused to marry me, even after I put a ring on your finger. You wasted my time and embarrassed me to my friends and family. You owe me. I need something from you."

As twisted as his logic was, Tristan wasn't going to leave until he said what he'd come to say, so Olivia might as well just get it over with. "Just tell me what it is..."

Instead of answering, he asked, "Who was that guy you were with at the restaurant?"

Axel's image flooded her mind again. Before Olivia realized what she was about to say, she blurted, "He's my fiancé."

*Fiancé? Really, Olivia?*

But she had nothing else to protect herself with. Maybe Tristan would think twice before putting his hands on her again if he knew she had a relationship with someone willing to stand up for her.

Maybe.

Especially if that relationship was with a man who couldn't be intimidated. Who would fight for her to the end—at least, that was the impression she'd gotten from Axel tonight.

Tristan didn't say anything for a moment. He only stared, an almost dumbfounded look in his eyes. "Your fiancé?"

"That's right. My fiancé." She felt a little more powerful as she said the words.

"You certainly didn't waste any time finding someone else, now did you?" Tristan's voice hardened with possessiveness, with disgust at her decision.

Her *fake* decision.

But he didn't need to know that.

Instead, Olivia raised her chin, determined to keep

going with this charade. "What can I say? When it's right, it's right."

He stared another moment until finally circling back around to his original statement. "I still need something from you."

"What's that?"

"You know how much my father loves you. He thinks you hung the moon, and he thinks I'm his loser offspring who can't do anything right."

Olivia couldn't argue with that assessment.

"If my father thinks you and I can still be friends after our breakup—that you still see something good in me even after all we went through—then maybe he'll think I actually can take over his company one day." Tristan stared at her as he waited for her response.

She blinked as she tried to comprehend his proposal. "You want me to be friendly with you around your father?"

"Yes. We have some events coming up this week. I want you to come. As my friend."

Olivia shook her head, baffled by the request. "You don't think he'll see through that? Your father is a very intelligent man."

"It's my best bet." Tristan frowned. "Especially considering the conversation I had with him this morning. I miss one meeting, and now he's saying I'm only good for working in the mailroom at the company. I need to do something to redeem myself."

Olivia thought about it a moment before shaking her head. The idea of getting Tristan off her back was tempting . . . but she didn't believe anything he said. There would always be something he wanted.

"I don't owe you anything, Tristan. You threatened me earlier tonight. You showed up inside my place. That's not okay. I need you to leave." She pointed at the door.

Tristan grabbed her arm again, tightening his grip until she yelped. "So help me, Olivia . . . if you don't do this, I'll tell everyone your secret. People around here . . . they won't think you're quite the good, wholesome girl you portray yourself to be."

Olivia sucked in a breath as she imagined that playing out. She had no doubt he'd ruin her reputation at the first chance—and he would use that as a way of manipulating her. The fallout would destroy the new life she'd begun to build in Lantern Beach.

She couldn't let that happen. "You wouldn't . . ."

His eyes glimmered. "I would. You know I'll do anything to get what I want."

That's how it had been with Tristan, hadn't it? He'd pursued Olivia hard until he won her over. When she realized his controlling ways and had tried to leave him, he'd then done everything in his power to keep her.

It was a game to him, a way of always trying to have the upper hand.

"So what's it going to be?" Tristan stared at her with his cold, lifeless eyes.

Her heart pattered in her chest. She just wanted this man out of her life once and for all.

But that didn't seem like reality...

However, there was always Axel... Olivia needed to play up her fake engagement. That was her way out of this. It was all she had right now, for that matter.

"Like I told you . . . I'm engaged." Her voice sounded scratchy, despite how she willed it not to. "It would be strange to go to your events when I'm with someone else."

"Bring him with you."

Her cheeks flushed. It would be hard to do that, considering they weren't really engaged.

Tristan leaned closer. "The first event, a little party, is tomorrow night."

She opened her mouth, wanting to argue. But no words left her lips. Instead, anxiety felt like it tried to strangle her.

Tristan rattled off the address.

"I'll see you there." He glared at her one more time as he paused with one hand on the door. "Oh, and you might want to tell your new fiancé to watch his steps."

At the words, truth hit her.

Without realizing what she'd done, Olivia had set up Axel as a target.

She sucked in a breath before quickly concealing the action.

She couldn't let Tristan know she'd lied. Couldn't give him any indication. That would give him another stronghold over her—one that just might break her.

Still, what had she been thinking telling him she was engaged?

It had been a terrible idea.

But it was too late to take her statement back now.

---

AXEL PAUSED as he stepped into the conference room at the Blackout headquarters. He'd been called to an emergency meeting with his team and, unfortunately, he was late.

It was all thanks to that driver who'd cut him off.

Thankfully, his bike wasn't damaged. He'd been able to pull it out of the ditch and head back as planned.

But his clothes had been covered with mud and dank-smelling swamp water. He had a small cut on his forehead. And he was cranky about it all.

People really needed to share the road with bikers.

He pushed those thoughts out of his mind as he turned toward his team.

Colton Locke—the co-founder and director of Blackout—stood at the front of the room. Seated around the table was team leader Rocco Foster, Beckett "No Smile" Jones, and rookie Gabe Michaels.

Axel scowled when he saw an image on the screen behind Colton. He dropped into an empty leather chair and stared, his curiosity growing by the moment.

"What's that guy's picture doing up there?" He nodded at the picture, feeling red-hot anger surge through his veins again.

He'd never forget what that man looked like.

Tristan.

That's what Olivia said his name was.

Right now, a headshot of him with that untouchable smile on his face was about all Axel could take. The man had sandy-brown hair that was brushed away from his forehead and short on the sides. He had bulky muscles and a thick neck. His tan looked like it came from a bottle, and his clothes probably cost more than Axel made in a week.

So why had Axel's team put up this guy's picture for their meeting?

"He's involved in the case we're working," Colton said.

Axel shifted in his chair. Certainly he hadn't heard correctly. "You mean the investigation into Oasis Management Systems?"

It was the only assignment on their docket for this

week.

"Exactly." Rocco's jaw flexed as he examined Axel. "Why does it seem like he's familiar to you?"

"Because he is." Axel rubbed his jaw as he recalled tonight's events. "That guy went after a waitress at Lisa's place. The woman—Olivia—said he didn't hit her, but he was on the verge of seriously hurting her."

A knot formed in his chest at the memory.

Beckett turned toward him. "Glad you got there when you did. You actually talked to this guy?"

"I tried." Axel pointed to the screen, reading the words at the bottom of the image. "*He's* a part of the Oasis Management Group?"

They'd already gone through a list of employees, and Axel had an excellent memory for faces. The man who'd cornered Olivia tonight hadn't been on that list.

Colton's jaw flexed as he glanced at Tristan's picture again. "That's right. We didn't think he was involved in the company's leadership. His name wasn't on the list Bart Jennings originally gave us. But the man is here in Lantern Beach. Since his father runs the company, it's a possibility he's being groomed to take over one day."

Axel crossed his arms and leaned back in his chair. He hadn't expected this turn of events—and he didn't like it. "What do you know about him?"

"Name is Tristan Bennett," Colton said. "He's thirty-two years old. His father is Stan Bennett, owner of Oasis Management Systems, which, as you know, operates computer systems for various hotel chains throughout the company."

So Olivia's ex-fiancé just happened to be here on Lantern Beach—the very place she'd come—on a business trip.

The coincidence seemed sketchy to Axel.

Bart Jennings, the CEO of one of the hotel chains associated with Oasis, believed this computer program was somehow being used to target certain women who'd been abducted. He'd talked to the local police in Philadelphia, where he lived, but they hadn't taken him seriously.

That's when Bart had hired Blackout to investigate. He'd given Oasis the opportunity to go anywhere on a corporate retreat paid for by Green Springs Hotels as their way of saying thank you for the business.

Blackout hadn't encouraged them to come to Lantern Beach. Quite the opposite, actually. The island had seen more than its fair share of crimes throughout the years. They definitely didn't want to bring in more trouble, and the team had been prepared to travel to whatever location necessary to do their job.

But Oasis had picked Lantern Beach, of all places. They hadn't known about Blackout or their presence here.

It had seemed strange. The whole team admitted that. But Lantern Beach *was* a popular tourist destination.

"Why do you have Tristan Bennett's picture up as opposed to other board members?" Gabe Michaels twirled a pencil in his hands as he waited for an answer.

"Just in case he's the ringleader instead of his father," Colton said. "All along, our plan has been to get a foothold into the company by infiltrating their social gatherings. As you know, we'll be dressing as waitstaff to work their parties. When we do, you'll sneak away to access their computers and see if you can find out anything while the rest of us distract the key players."

Beckett raked a hand through his hair. "I'm still not clear why we needed this last-minute meeting. We already have all this planned out."

"We didn't anticipate Tristan being here," Colton said. "Sources tell us he's into some shady stuff and that he has a violent past. Everyone is going to need to watch their backs."

It looked like Axel might have another excuse to talk to Olivia again after all.

As he remembered her icy glare, he wasn't sure if he looked forward to that . . . or dreaded it.

Either way, the most important thing was that she stayed safe.

And knowing what he did about Tristan's ties to Oasis . . . that task had just become a lot harder.

## CHAPTER SIX

OLIVIA HARDLY SLEPT at all during the night. She couldn't stop thinking about Tristan being on the island. In her apartment. At her place of employment.

Nor could she stop thinking about the fact she'd told him she was engaged to Axel.

Now Axel might be in danger.

She might not like the man, but that didn't mean she wished any harm on him either.

Her mind remained on the situation as she worked in The Crazy Chefette's kitchen, chopping some green onions. Even though she was a waitress, she helped as sous chef if things got slow in the dining room. It didn't happen very often, but there were lulls on occasion—like right now. It was still a little too early for the breakfast rush.

As she chopped, she mulled things over. Olivia *had*

to figure out how to handle this situation. But no matter which way she looked at it, no good solutions came to mind.

If she told Tristan the truth, he'd leverage it over her.

If she didn't tell him the truth, Axel could be hurt.

"Are you okay?" Lisa paused beside her, depositing a basket full of fresh vegetables on the stainless-steel counter. "Using a knife while you're distracted is never a good thing. I use a lot of strange ingredients, but I don't plan on making fingers one of them."

Olivia placed the knife on the cutting board and swallowed hard. Lisa was right.

Olivia had been chopping away, but her mind had been in a different place.

She wished she and Lisa were better friends. If they were, Olivia might pour out all her problems to her. But that didn't seem appropriate to do with her boss, no matter how tempting.

"I was just thinking about Axel." Olivia wiped her hands on a paper towel as she turned to Lisa. "I wanted to thank him for stepping in yesterday."

Lisa began to unload and rinse the vegetables in the sink. "I know he can come across as being a little arrogant, I suppose. Or maybe full of himself. But he's actually not a bad guy."

Olivia tried to hide the doubt from showing on her face. She found it hard to believe Axel wasn't the womanizing, arrogant man she'd assumed—even if he *had* saved her from Tristan last night. She knew his type all too well.

Instead, Olivia forced herself to smile and nod. She didn't want to insult or offend her boss. "Good to know."

Lisa nodded toward the dining area. "Speak of the devil... it looks like it's your lucky day."

Olivia glanced through the opening into the dining area just as Axel stepped inside.

This was early for him. He usually came at dinner time.

"Listen, we're not busy yet," Lisa said. "Why don't you take a ten-minute break and talk to him? Maybe that will help curtail your distraction before we have to file a workman's comp claim."

Despite the sickly feeling growing in Olivia's stomach, she nodded. "Okay. I will. Thank you."

She took off her apron and left it in the kitchen area.

Then she swallowed hard as she prepared to confess what she'd done to Axel.

---

THE HOSTESS HAD SEATED Axel at his normal booth. He'd just picked up his menu when he spotted the person he was looking for.

Olivia.

The fact was, he hadn't come here for breakfast. He'd come to find out when her shift started.

The pretty waitress started toward him, what appeared to be a pleasant smile plastered on her face.

In all the times Axel had been coming here, the woman had only scowled at him every time he looked her way.

He found it halfway amusing. She clearly thought he was a player, but he wasn't. Not at all. In fact, he hadn't dated anyone since Mandy.

Sometimes, he didn't think he ever wanted to give love a try again.

He might be a risk-taker, but not when it came to his heart.

Olivia paused by his table, looking tense despite her smile. The woman really was gorgeous. Her hair fell to her shoulders, her features were gentle, and her figure . . . well, it was just right.

"I'm glad you're here." She jutted a hip out as she stood beside his table.

"You are?" Her statement was suspicious in itself. What had caused this change of heart? Last time they'd spoken, she'd been colder than the Arctic.

In winter.

During La Niña.

She ran her hands down the side of her jeans, as if her palms might be sweaty, and nibbled on her bottom lip before finally asking, "Any chance I could grab a few minutes alone with you?"

"You don't have to thank me again."

Her smile dipped. "That's good because I wasn't going to."

Axel hid his smile. She was direct. He liked that.

"Good to know." He murmured thanks to the hostess as she delivered a cup of coffee to the table.

Olivia waited until the woman disappeared before nodding.

She wanted to talk somewhere else.

This should be interesting.

Axel rose from his booth. He'd have to get a fresh cup of coffee later.

He followed Olivia outside into the parking lot. As they stepped onto the sidewalk at the side of the building, he scanned their surroundings.

The vehicles. The dumpster. Even the houses in the background.

He saw no signs of trouble.

Olivia leaned against the pink, cedar-shingled wall. Her actions showed she was nervous. Her gaze darted back and forth. Her motions appeared jerky. Her skin shone with perspiration.

Axel's curiosity grew.

"Look, this is awkward." She rubbed her throat as if it was tight. "But there's something I need to tell you."

"What's that?" Axel stepped back, anxious to hear what she had to say.

Her gaze fluttered up to meet his. "Tristan showed up at my place last night. He'd somehow gotten inside and was waiting for me when I got home."

Any of Axel's earlier amusement disappeared as his muscles bristled. He didn't like the sound of that. He knew he should have insisted on following her home and checking out her place. But he also knew it wouldn't have been welcome.

"Did he hurt you?" His gaze swept over her, looking for any signs Olivia had been harmed.

He saw nothing—thankfully. But that didn't mean she wasn't hiding her injuries.

Olivia quickly shook her head as she tugged at her sleeve. "No, it wasn't like that. But . . . he asked about who you were."

Axel's shoulders relaxed—but only slightly. "Okay . . ."

"I don't know what I was thinking. Because I never meant to pull you into this." She rubbed her throat again.

"What did you tell him?" Axel's curiosity continued to spike. He couldn't even imagine where she was going with this.

She nibbled on her bottom lip a moment before blurting, "I don't know why I did it, but I told him that you're my fiancé."

Axel's eyebrows shot up. "Your fiancé?"

"I know it sounds crazy. I just thought if Tristan thought I was engaged to someone who was able to handle himself—and someone strong enough to scare away Tristan—maybe he would leave me alone."

Any other time, Axel actually might take a moment to revel in the fact Olivia had just called him strong and maybe even intimidating. But this wasn't the time or place.

Instead, he crossed his arms and observed Olivia a moment. "Okay, so you told him we were engaged. What's the problem?"

She nibbled on her bottom lip again. "I'm afraid he might come after you. I didn't even think about it when I was talking, and the words just came out. Now, I don't know what to do. I can call him back and tell him that I made it up—"

"No, don't do that." Axel readjusted his stance, bringing his hands to his waist as a surge of protectiveness rose in him. "That will just give him more ammunition against you."

Olivia stared up at him, uncertainty in her gaze. "Are you sure? I don't know how long he's going to be on the island and—"

"He'll be here for a week."

She froze before slowly tilting her head. She sounded almost breathless as she asked, "How do you know that?"

"It's a long story."

Her earlier apology-laced nervousness disappeared as she bristled.

She crossed her arms now and offered a hard stare. "I've got time."

## CHAPTER SEVEN

AXEL FELT Olivia's haunches rise and knew if he didn't act quickly that the wall between them would only grow higher and stronger. "I haven't been looking into you, if that's what you think."

The same skeptical look remained in her eyes. "So . . . ?"

He let out a breath, wondering how much he could say. He couldn't assume that he could trust Olivia, even though his gut told him he could.

Still, he and the guys had come up with a cover story. That way, even if Olivia betrayed them, the guys from Oasis wouldn't know the truth.

"My team is investigating his company," he finally said.

Olivia stared at him another moment before shaking her head. "What does that even mean?"

"I work for Blackout, a private—"

"Security firm made up of former Navy SEALs," she finished, looking unimpressed.

Axel raised his eyebrows. "You been looking into me?"

She scowled, clearly not appreciating his playful humor.

"Hardly. I heard some women talking about it. About *you*." She gave him a pointed look that clearly said she wasn't at all captivated with either his career or that he was a topic of conversation among the ladies.

Axel thought her reaction was cute—but this wasn't the time to show that.

"Anyway, my team was hired to investigate his business," he said. "We believe they may be involved with . . . identity theft."

"Identity theft?"

He shrugged. "It's a big business."

She tilted her head as her eyes narrowed. "You mean, it really *is* a coincidence Tristan is here at the same time I am? That this just happened to be where they planned their retreat?"

Axel offered a half shrug. "That's how it appears."

Olivia's eyes narrowed even more. "What other kind of shady things are they doing?"

"I can't tell you that. But, if our hunches are correct, these guys will be going away for a long time."

Her eyes brightened as her gaze locked with his. "Let me help."

Axel twisted his head. He hadn't expected *that*. "You helping sounds like a terrible idea."

Olivia stepped closer, not losing any of her determination. "I want to bring Tristan down. I'm the connection you need to get into the Oasis events."

"We have guys who are going to be disguised as wait staff. That should be plenty."

"But Tristan told me he wanted me to be there. He even said I could bring my fiancé."

Axel's breath caught. *That* was an interesting idea. Maybe it could even be the "in" they were looking for.

Then he shook his head. "Still a terrible idea."

He couldn't possibly let Olivia entertain the thought of helping infiltrate. It was too dangerous.

Especially when he remembered how she'd looked yesterday when she'd been on the ground near the dumpster.

Axel had let this conversation go on for too long already.

Now it was time for him to get going.

The team was headed to the retreat later today, and Axel needed to get ready for it.

When he heard Olivia suck in a quick breath, he froze.

Something was wrong.

"OLIVIA . . . ?"

Olivia pulled her gaze from the woods and back toward Axel. "What?"

He stiffened as he stood in front of her, his stance changing from relaxed to protective. "What's going on?"

"I feel like . . ." She frowned, knowing how her words would come across.

"What do you feel like?" he prodded.

"I know I'm going to sound crazy. But I feel like someone is watching us right now."

Axel stepped closer, his gaze scanning their surroundings. "I don't see anyone."

Olivia pulled her arms across her chest. "I don't either. But I can't shake the feeling."

She surveyed everything around her. The cars. A patch of trees. Innumerable houses.

But she didn't see anything out of place.

Still, could someone be hiding behind one of those windows? The morning sun hit the panes, causing a glare. Anyone could watch them from there, and they wouldn't be able to see.

Or was she just paranoid?

Was that note she'd received messing with her mind?

Axel took one last glance behind them before

gently gripping her arm. "Let's get you back inside. Then I need to run."

Panic rushed through Olivia at the thought.

He couldn't leave. Not yet.

She needed to get Tristan out of her life for good. What better way to do that than putting him behind bars? Then he couldn't hurt her anymore.

How could she convince Axel of that without spilling all her secrets?

As soon as they stepped back into the safety of the restaurant, she turned toward him, keeping her voice low.

"Tristan's dad, Stan . . . he adores me," she blurted. "That's why Tristan told me—I mean, asked me—to go with him to some of Oasis's events. He wants me to 'work my magic.' And if I don't go . . ."

Axel stared at Olivia, his eyes studying her every expression without apology. "Then what?"

The words almost sounded breathless as they left his lips.

Olivia swallowed hard, wishing she didn't have to go there. But Axel had left her with no choice. "Then Tristan will make my life miserable."

Axel's gaze darkened. "He said that?"

"Not in so many words. But, yes, he did. With or without you, I'm going to end up at that party tonight."

Axel swung his head back and forth, all playfulness gone. "Olivia, that sounds like a bad idea."

"So go with me. Stan will be much more inclined to talk to you if I'm with you. It will seem more natural if you start asking questions."

Axel continued to stare. "You're serious?"

Olivia nodded. "Dead serious."

He let out a long breath, worry still staining his gaze. "Olivia . . . I don't think you realize how dangerous this could be."

She touched her arm, rubbing the area where a bruise had formed from when Tristan grabbed her. "Believe me, I do."

Axel said nothing for another moment. Instead, his jaw flexed. His eyes flickered. His muscles tightened. "You're really going to go with or without me?"

"I don't have much choice."

"You always have a choice, Olivia." His voice sounded low and serious.

Something about his tone made a shiver go up her spine.

Olivia wished she could explain. Wished she could spill everything. About Tristan. About the secret he held over her.

But she couldn't. She knew the revelation would only paint her in a negative light.

Besides, she'd come to Lantern Beach to hit that reset button in her life. If people believed what Tristan told them about her . . . then she'd be forced to leave. To start again.

That was the last thing she wanted.

"Give me some time to figure out things," Axel finally said. "I need to talk to my guys about your idea and get back with you. But, for the record, I still think it's a terrible idea. You could be putting yourself in the line of fire. Plus, I don't like the idea of you being around that guy."

Olivia swallowed hard.

She knew she was only acting out of desperation.

That very desperation would keep her reputation intact . . . or get her killed.

"One more thing . . ." Axel locked his gaze with hers. "How would you feel about me helping you change the lock on your door?"

## CHAPTER EIGHT

AXEL COULDN'T BELIEVE that Olivia had said yes.

While he'd run to the store to pick up some supplies, Olivia had requested her lunch break and had said she'd meet him at her apartment in thirty.

Sure enough, as soon as he walked up a flight of stairs at her complex, Axel spotted Olivia pulling out her keys near her front door.

Axel didn't miss how she shoved a white paper into her pocket as she turned to him, looking a little more unsettled than she had before.

"Did something happen?" he asked.

She shook her head a little too quickly. "No, why?"

"Just checking." He held up his bag. "I think I have what I need."

"Perfect. I'll pay you back for anything that you bought."

He wasn't all that concerned about money.

She shoved her key in the lock and pushed the door open. She froze in the doorway and glanced around.

Again, Axel sensed that something was wrong.

Should he even ask again?

He peered over her shoulder, expecting to see something had happened. Expecting to see that her apartment had been ransacked.

But everything looked fine.

"Olivia?"

Without looking back at him, she murmured, "I think somebody has been inside."

---

"STAY HERE," Axel muttered.

Olivia didn't argue. She had no desire to step any further into her apartment.

Especially not after that note she'd just found. The one that read, *We're meant to be together. I can't wait until you realize it too. In the meantime, I'm here if you need me. Always close. Always listening. Always there for you.*

She'd shoved it into her pocket before Axel could see it and ask questions.

A moment later, Axel returned and shook his head. "It's clear."

"That's a relief." And it was. But Olivia still couldn't shake that feeling.

"Is there something specific that made you feel off-kilter like this?"

She shook her head. "I can't put my finger on it. It's just this feeling I have that something's wrong."

"If it makes you feel better, nobody's here."

She nodded and shoved a hair behind her ear, trying not to show just how frightened she felt.

"I'm sure it's just everything that has happened. It's all messing with my head."

"I understand. Let me get this new lock installed for you. Maybe it will give you some peace of mind."

She knew that it would. But the question was, would it give her enough peace of mind?

Could Tristan have left that note? Last night, he'd seemed more interested in getting what he needed from her than winning her back.

But if it wasn't Tristan, who could it be?

## CHAPTER NINE

AXEL SENSED there was something Olivia wasn't telling him. And the truth was, she had no obligation to spill anything to him. But he was curious about this woman.

"So where are you from?" he asked as he unscrewed the doorknob.

She stood against the wall, drinking a sweaty glass of water. She'd offered him some also, but he told her he was fine.

"Kentucky."

"Kentucky? What part?"

"Lexington."

"UK, huh?"

"To the end."

He smiled. "You a big basketball fan?"

He wanted to keep her talking and learn a little bit more about her in the process.

"My dad used to take me to the games. I have a lot of good memories of that."

"Your parents still live there?"

"They actually moved down to Florida a couple of years ago. My mom was having some problems with her asthma so she headed south to see if that would help."

"Brothers and sisters?"

"I'm an only child. My parents raised me to be independent, so I've pretty much been on my own ever since I graduated from high school."

"Did you go to the University of Kentucky? I had a good friend in the military who went there."

Olivia took a long sip of her water before nodding. "I did. I studied marketing."

"And you ended up here working at a restaurant?" He tried to put the pieces together in his mind.

"It's a long story."

Axel was curious to know what that long story was about. But he wouldn't push.

"I just need to do a couple more things and this door should be good to go." He knew she didn't have much time until she had to get back to work.

As she stood there, her gaze suddenly narrowed. "How did you get that scratch on the side of your forehead?"

As Axel remembered last night's incident, he frowned.

She wasn't the only one who had things that she didn't want to talk about.

---

OLIVIA SAW the shadow form over Axel's gaze.

He touched the area at his forehead. It hadn't been there last night. Olivia would have remembered.

But it *had* been there this morning. She just hadn't said anything about it until now. Her overthinking brain had been working overtime.

"It's nothing," he said.

Clearly, that wasn't the truth. It was something. What had happened in the time between when Axel had helped her last night and today?

Before she could ask any more questions, he stood. He closed the door to make sure it would latch and then opened it again.

"Now let me test the key," he muttered.

Good. A change of subject.

Olivia watched as he stepped outside. A moment later, the door opened.

Axel smiled as he held the key out to her. "All done. Here you go."

"I really appreciate you taking the time to do this."

"It's no problem. You need to be able to get a good night's rest, don't you?"

"I'll never complain about a good night's rest." She shifted. "I guess you haven't had time to talk to your guys about me helping you."

It had been all she had been thinking about since she made the offer. A part of her wanted to withdraw it, another part of her felt a surge of excitement like she hadn't felt in a long time.

If Tristan was doing something wrong, Olivia wanted to help bring him down. She knew that vengeance was the Lord's, but she also knew that some people deserved more justice than others.

People like Tristan.

"Once I leave here, I'll talk to the guys about it."

"Thank you."

She knew she wouldn't be able to concentrate the rest of the day as she waited to hear what they said.

## CHAPTER TEN

AS ROCCO LIFTED weights inside the Blackout gym, Axel helped spot him. Axel was anxious to tell his leader about his conversation with Olivia—and about Olivia's proposal.

But Rocco beat him to the start. "Dan Marxon is dead."

Axel blanched as he hovered close to the weight bench in case Rocco needed him. "What? The CEO of Vacation Inn Hotels?"

Rocco grunted as he lifted the barbell again. "He's the one."

"What happened?"

"He was shot while jogging in a park early this morning."

Axel shook his head, still reeling with disbelief. "Do they know who did it?"

"They're blaming it on a local gang. I have my doubts."

"So my other question is: does this have to do with our case?"

"That's my best guess. I suspect Marxon got suspicious of Oasis but that he wasn't as quiet about that fact as Bart Jennings has been."

Axel rubbed his jaw as the layers continued to unfold, each one bringing a new, startling level of danger with it. "I thought this was going to be a pretty simple case. Maybe it's not."

Rocco set the barbell back into its cradle before sitting up and grabbing a towel to wipe his face. "What did you want to talk to me about?"

Axel hesitated a moment before telling him about Olivia's proposal and how unsettled he felt about it. When he finished, Rocco stared at him a moment before shaking his head.

"You're right. That does sound like a terrible idea. She's a civilian and could get hurt."

"I agree. But Olivia is going to this party with or without me. I don't know her well enough to talk her out of it, and she seems pretty determined. There's obviously more history here than she's telling me."

Rocco's jaw flexed as he narrowed his gaze. "You think this guy is holding something over her?"

Axel shrugged. "That's my best guess. She said he could make her life miserable. I have no idea what this could be about, but she's motivated to follow through."

Rocco sighed and wiped his face again. In five hours, the rest of Axel's team would head toward the beachfront mansion where the Oasis retreat was taking place. They'd act as servers at a dinner party this evening.

"I'm just saying, Olivia already has an 'in' with Stan, the CEO of Oasis, *and* his son Tristan. What she said was correct. These guys will be much more likely to open up to somebody they know than they would to a server offering shrimp cocktail. While you guys try to crack the code on their computer, I can see what I can find out by talking to them."

Rocco frowned. "I don't want to put her in danger. She obviously has a bad history with these people. Even if she's physically safe with us, I'm not sure how this could emotionally affect her."

Axel had thought of that too. "Neither do I. Believe me, I don't. It's clear that she's already shaken. I don't want her to get hurt any further. But if she's going to attend this event with or without me, I will feel better if I'm able to stick close to her."

Rocco stood and turned toward Axel, crossing his arms over his chest. "She actually told this guy that the two of you were engaged?"

"I guess she thought it might keep him away from her. It's not that I want to use circumstances to our advantage . . . but it seems like a shame to waste the opportunity. It's like the perfect door has opened. And I won't let her get hurt."

"Is she . . . fragile?"

Axel remembered the fire he'd seen in her eyes. "She was scared yesterday when he cornered her. But I wouldn't call her fragile. She's got a fighting spirit."

Rocco thought about it for a moment before nodding. "Okay then. Let's do it. Do you think this woman can meet with us so we can brief her?"

"I'll give Lisa a call and see if I can get up with Olivia."

"Good. Because the two of you are going to need to come up with a cover story—especially if you want these guys to buy that you're actually engaged. You're also going to need a ring."

Axel swallowed hard. He'd thought of that. And he had a solution. It wasn't a good one, but it was the only thing that made sense right now.

"I have Mandy's old one." His throat burned as he said the words. "I'll see if it fits."

Rocco paused, surprise washing through his gaze as he studied him. "Are you sure you want to do that?"

"I'm sure. It will be a nice reminder of exactly why I don't ever want to be in a serious relationship again."

"Axel—"

"And please don't take that as an excuse to tell me how happy you are right now with Peyton." Axel threw his friend a knowing smile. "I know you guys are as happy as two kids in a cupcake shop. Everybody from miles around can see it, for that matter. But that kind of relationship isn't for me."

Rocco straightened. "If that's what you say."

Axel stepped toward the door, not bothering to respond. "I'm going to call Lisa. If this arrangement is going to happen, then we need to get this show on the road."

"Two more things, Axel," Rocco said.

Axel paused and glanced back. "What's that?"

"Someone named Kiki called and left a message for you. She wants you to call her back."

Axel's cheeks heated. She'd called Blackout trying to reach him? She had a lot of nerve. Too much. Too much persistence.

That wasn't okay.

But Axel didn't want Rocco to know that.

He nodded, keeping his expression level. "Good to know. Second thing?"

Rocco locked gazes with him. "Don't break the waitress's heart."

Axel nearly snorted.

He had no intention of doing that. He had no intention of stealing her heart either.

Sure, the woman was gorgeous. But Axel meant it when he said he never wanted to dive deep into a relationship again.

Plus, now he needed to deal with Kiki...

---

OLIVIA COULDN'T HELP but look over her shoulder the rest of her shift at work.

That earlier feeling of being watched wouldn't leave her.

Nor would the fact that she'd agreed to go to that party tonight and pretend to be friendly with Tristan. How was she ever going to pull that off? Especially with Axel as her pretend fiancé?

She didn't know. Right now, she needed to concentrate on her job.

She smiled as she approached a man sitting alone at a table. Instead of wearing typical beach garb, he wore jeans and a white button-up shirt. His hairline was beginning to fade, and glasses perched on his nose. Olivia would guess him to be a few years older than she was.

The man offered a tentative smile as she approached.

"Welcome to The Crazy Chefette." She paused by his table. "What can I get for you?"

He glanced at the laminated menu and frowned. "It's my first time here. What do you recommend?"

"The grilled cheese with peaches is always a hit."

He raised his eyebrows and glanced at her, not

bothering to hide his skepticism. "That's not something I would have ever considered. But you say it's good?"

"I love it." Olivia really did. It was the perfect blend of sweet and savory. People came from all over to try it.

He closed his menu and nodded. "Okay then. I'm going to trust your recommendation. I'll try one."

"You won't regret it." Olivia jotted his order down on her pad. "Anything to drink?"

"Sweet ice tea."

"You got it." She turned to walk away.

"Excuse me," he called.

She paused and turned back toward him. "Yes?"

"Are you from around here?"

Her muscles tightened. Was this man just being polite? Or was there more to this conversation?

Olivia licked her lips. "I'm not. What do you need?"

"Just looking for some recommendations of things to do while I'm in town."

She glanced at his jeans and his stiff posture, trying to put together a better picture of the man. "Where are you from?"

"Connecticut. I'm down here on business."

"Well, I think I have a simple answer to your question. The beach."

He let out a small chuckle. "I should have known you'd say that. But what if I don't like sand?"

She laughed at his apologetic expression. "Then I'd

say you have a problem. I'm sorry to say there are no theaters or even bumper cars around here. People come here for the Atlantic, plain and simple."

"At least I can try out some good food while I'm in town, I suppose. Good food with good service."

Based on the look he gave her, Olivia knew what he was getting at. He'd be back to the restaurant to see her. She'd had enough guys hit on her to know when it happened, whether overtly or subtly.

She remembered what she'd vowed earlier this week.

That she wanted a boring man who worked behind a desk and who was terrible at flirting.

This man fit the bill.

Then Olivia remembered she was supposed to be engaged to Axel.

Her thoughts clashed inside.

It didn't matter.

She had more important things than romance to worry about.

"You hold tight, sir," she said. "I'll be right back with your order."

## CHAPTER ELEVEN

AXEL FROWNED as he jogged down the road with Rocco.

After Rocco had finished lifting weights, he'd asked Axel to go on a run with him. Training and staying fit were part of their job. They needed to stay strong in order to carry out their operations.

Running usually helped Axel to clear his head. But right now, he continued to mentally review this case. He wanted to be familiar with every aspect of what was going on here.

For that reason, he'd rehashed the profiles of the victims.

Each were attractive. In their twenties. They had good backgrounds and people who cared about them.

Normal victims of human trafficking were girls or women with no one who would miss them.

These women didn't fit that profile.

In fact, *Olivia* seemed to fit the profile of the women who'd gone missing.

Axel tensed at the thought.

Each of them had checked into the hotel alone. Three had gone out that evening to the hotel bar downstairs. Two had talked to men while they'd been there. Both of those men had been cleared.

The next morning, the women had been discovered missing. Security footage at the hotel showed nothing—empty hallways.

But that didn't seem possible.

If these women had been abducted, how had they been taken from their hotel rooms without anyone seeing? It didn't make sense.

Not only that, but it was disturbing.

The FBI was also working this case, but Bart had hired Blackout because he wanted his own investigation into things—especially since his hotel's reputation was on the line. He said that at one point he and Stan had been close. Stan still thought they were close, but Bart was distancing himself from the man, feeling uneasy about this turn of events.

So far, none of the victims had been found.

They only knew that someone had heard chatter that a woman from Lantern Beach was next.

Wherever Stan Bennett went, that seemed to be where women disappeared.

And the man was on the island this week.

Rocco answered a call on his Bluetooth earbud and muttered a few things before turning to Axel. "I've got an update."

"What's going on?" Axel tried to push the bothersome thoughts from his mind. As he did, his vision blurred a moment and he rubbed his eyes.

"Still having problems?" Rocco squinted as he glanced at him, the two of them keeping a steady pace beside each other.

"Unfortunately. I went to the eye doctor, and he couldn't find anything wrong."

"Between your blurry vision and my migraines, we're falling apart."

"We're too young to fall apart."

Axel realized precisely the unspoken conversations that lingered.

Ever since their Seal team had been involved in something called Operation Grandiose, they'd all had problems. The mission had been one of the most intense of their careers. In the middle of battle, the enemy had sprayed some type of unidentified chemical on them. Now, each of them had ailments.

"Anyway, back to that update," Rocco said. "I finally got up with Lucas."

Axel straightened. "And?"

"He's fine. He was out of the country for a while, but now he's back."

Axel released his breath. "That's good news."

Two other men who had been on that mission with them—John and Quinn—had recently died in mysterious accidents. The rest of the team feared something might be going on. But everything had been quiet for the past month, leading them to believe that maybe it was a coincidence.

Axel sucked in a breath as a new thought hit him.

But, before he could speak the words aloud, an explosion filled the air.

---

OLIVIA CUT her shift early and went to her apartment.

She needed to shower to get the scent of food off her before she headed to her briefing at Blackout. But she still had a few minutes to unwind before she did that.

She paused near a surfboard she'd bought when she moved here. Olivia figured she could at least learn to catch some waves while she was here. But doing it by herself just didn't seem like that much fun.

Eventually, she needed to figure out what her future looked like.

She had a degree in marketing. She loved developing print and online campaigns. As much as waitressing—and getting to know the people on the island

—had been a nice distraction, Olivia knew that wasn't something she wanted to do forever.

But how many opportunities for working a job in marketing were there here on this island?

She wasn't sure.

Olivia had come here because of good memories. She'd had family vacations here as a teen, and, when she'd been here, she hadn't wanted to leave. She hoped to recreate some of that now.

This turn of events, however, sent her plans spiraling.

She fixed herself a cup of coffee and sat on her couch. As she did, she pulled out the two notes she'd received and stared at them.

The messages sent a shiver down her spine.

*My love, you're so beautiful. I can't wait until we meet.*

*We're meant to be together. I can't wait until you realize it too. In the meantime, I'm here if you need me. Always close. Always listening. Always there for you.*

Had Tristan sent these?

Olivia frowned at the thought.

Part of her wanted to retreat. To run.

But her parents hadn't raised her to be a coward. That was why she'd ended her relationship with Tristan. She'd come to her senses after she'd seen his true colors.

Not that women who stayed in toxic relationships were cowards. Not at all. But Olivia had known she had the strength inside her, as well as the resources, to leave—so she had.

Tristan had never outwardly hit her.

But he'd threatened her. Intimidated her. Gaslighted her.

None of that was okay.

Which was precisely why she wanted to see him behind bars.

And she had good reason—reasons other than revenge.

Olivia had seen Tristan whispering to people. Had heard his secret phone calls. Seen the way he always had money, even when he didn't work.

He was involved with something illegal.

Olivia was certain of it.

But now she needed to find a way to prove it.

## CHAPTER TWELVE

AXEL AND ROCCO both dove out of the way of the blast.

Memories of war raged inside Axel as he smelled the burning. As he felt the heat. As he tasted blood in his mouth.

Each memory tried to swallow him.

But he couldn't let that happen.

Axel looked up in time to see the blaze die.

He glanced beside him at Rocco. His friend lifted his head toward the explosion, his eyes hardening.

"Are you okay?" Axel asked.

Rocco nodded, his cheeks still twitching as his entire body seemed to go on guard. "You?"

"Yeah." Axel stared at the fading flames. "What just happened?"

A bomb. That had been his first thought. But the blast radius hadn't been strong or large.

Rocco pulled himself to his feet and walked toward the source. Axel followed.

"It almost looks like a homemade firework. Fourth of July is coming up. You think . . . ?" Axel's voice trailed.

Rocco frowned as he stared at the charred black spot on the side of the road. "It's anyone's guess at this point. You think someone just happened to leave it here?"

The road was deserted. Other than the Blackout facility, the only other buildings nearby belonged to the community church a little farther down the road. Not many people came down this way past the church.

"It's seems like a little too much of a coincidence, doesn't it?" Axel asked.

Axel remembered what he'd been about to tell Rocco before the explosion.

When he put this incident together with what had happened yesterday . . .

Axel frowned.

"What?" Rocco squinted as he studied his face.

Axel touched the cut on the side of his forehead. "I got run off the road last night."

"What?" Rocco's voice rose. "Why didn't you say something?"

"Maybe I was a little embarrassed. I don't know. Really, it seemed like a freak accident but . . ."

"What if it wasn't?" Rocco finished for him.

Axel nodded slowly. "What if it wasn't?"

"You need to keep your eyes open. I don't like the sound of that."

"Me neither." Axel let out a breath. "I still have a bad feeling about involving Olivia in this . . ." Axel frowned as he thought about her.

What if she had been the one run off the road?

"She's our best chance," Rocco said. "But I agree. I don't want to see her get hurt."

"I fear she'll get hurt whether she's involved in this or not."

Axel's words hung in the air.

He wished he didn't believe they might be true.

But he did.

---

OLIVIA GLANCED AROUND as she drove through the security gate at the Blackout facility. She'd been buzzed in, and Axel was going to meet her out front of what he'd called the Daniel Oliver Building.

This place was massive.

Olivia had no idea when she'd first heard about the campus just how big an operation this was. A large lodge-like building stretched in the distance. An obstacle course could barely be seen on the other side, and she thought she caught a glimpse of the Pamlico Sound against the opposite edge of the property.

The entire compound was secured by a fence topped with razor wire.

A whisper of nerves raked through her. Somehow, seeing this place only drove home the seriousness of the situation. This wasn't a game. It wasn't a joke.

It was life or death.

She shuddered.

She pulled into the lot out front, and, as soon as she stepped from her vehicle, Axel emerged from the front door.

Her heart raced when she saw him.

Raced? That had to be nerves.

Olivia was simply on edge.

Who wouldn't be in a situation like this?

But the man was a sight to behold. There was nothing unappealing about him. At least, physically. Personality-wise was an entirely different story.

"You made it." Axel practically hopped down the steps to meet her. Each move was confident, like he was the kind of guy who always won, no matter what he did in life.

She was the type who'd always had to work hard to get what she wanted. She'd stayed up all night studying. She'd had to nurture friendships and work to earn people's trust.

Those things just came natural to Axel, didn't they?

Olivia frowned and stuffed her hands into the pockets of her jean shorts. "I did. I heard I needed to be briefed before the party tonight."

He nodded toward the door. "I'll give you a tour another time. Unfortunately, we don't have a lot of wiggle room right now."

Axel led the way into a conference room, introduced Olivia to the rest of the team, and then seated her at the front of the table.

Colton Locke, the leader of the group and someone Olivia had spoken with before at The Crazy Chefette, began showing her a slide show of who they were dealing with.

Pictures of various Oasis employees filled the screen. Olivia recognized almost everyone. She didn't know each one of them personally, but she'd seen them around the office when she worked there.

She frowned when Colton finished showing the photos, feeling more like she'd been given a high-level security briefing than a rundown on an ID theft operation. "This seems like a lot of trouble you guys are going through for identity theft."

The guys were quiet around her until finally Colton spoke. "That's one of the worries. But, Olivia, these men are dangerous. Very dangerous. If you're not comfortable—"

"I'm going to do this," she said. "No one can talk me

out of it. I just need to buy an appropriate dress and some shoes then I'll be good to go."

The guys glanced at each other again.

Finally, Colton nodded. "There's no time for shopping. I'll ask Elise to help with the outfit. We need to get your cover story in place and run over a few safety precautions..."

"The sooner we get this over with, the sooner we can get some sushi," Beckett said.

"Sushi?" What were they talking about?

Axel shook his head. "Ignore them. They have strange coping mechanisms. Don't they, Junior?" He turned to the youngest member of the group. Olivia thought his name was Gabe.

The man playfully scowled. "Strange coping mechanisms? Let me tell you how it all went down."

The men around her laughed.

Olivia was glad they could have their humor at a time like this. Their comradery was touching.

But she had other things on her mind—things that wouldn't let her forget, no matter how much she might want to.

## CHAPTER THIRTEEN

OLIVIA COULDN'T BELIEVE she was doing this. She fisted and unfisted her hands before shaking them out as last-minute jitters claimed her.

Had she lost her mind?

That was clearly the case. There was no other way to explain this.

If someone had asked Olivia last week if she'd be getting dressed up for a party her ex was attending and that she'd be heading there with a fake fiancé, she would have laughed.

Then again, this whole situation was no laughing matter.

"You look great."

Olivia turned back toward Elise Locke, the woman who'd loaned her a dress for the party and helped her get ready. Not that Olivia needed help getting ready for a party. But it was nice to have another female around to give opinions.

Besides, Olivia hadn't exactly brought any dress clothes with her when she came to Lantern Beach. She'd practically left with just the clothes on her back but had slowly added to what she had.

She glanced in the mirror and raised her eyebrows with surprise at the final result of her pampering.

Elise had let her borrow a beautiful blue sundress. The outfit was modest and classy, but it definitely made a statement.

Olivia hadn't felt this pretty in a long time. Probably not since the first few dates she'd gone on with Tristan. He'd charmed her by taking her to the nicest restaurants and making her feel like a million bucks. He'd been so complimentary that she'd felt like she was walking on clouds.

Too bad none of it was real.

Elise had even helped her to curl her hair so that the strands flowed in soft waves down to her shoulders and her makeup was just enough to make her look elegant but light enough to feel natural.

"Thank you for your help." She smiled at Elise.

The woman had a short, dark hairstyle that fit her pert face. Plus, based on her growing belly, she was expecting a baby in a few months. Olivia didn't ask, and Elise didn't volunteer the information. She had told Olivia that she was a psychologist and married to Colton Locke.

"It's no problem." Elise started to grin, but her smile faded when she glanced at Olivia's arm. "What happened there?"

Olivia rubbed the bruise Tristan had given her. She thought she'd covered it up with some makeup, but apparently the concealer had faded. "It's nothing."

Elise narrowed her eyes. "It doesn't look like nothing."

"I . . . I don't really want to talk about it." Olivia didn't want to make excuses for Tristan, nor did she want to explain. She knew Tristan had treated her wrong. On all counts.

That was why it was even more important that she help put him behind bars.

"Understood. Be careful tonight. But remember to also enjoy spending time with your fiancé."

Olivia nearly snorted. "Pretend fiancé. And that's going to be a challenge."

"Why? Axel is a nice guy."

"Nice guy or not . . . love—or anything that resembles love—isn't for me."

"I thought that after my first husband died."

Olivia froze. "Your first husband?"

Elise stepped back and nodded. "This building was named after him. Daniel Oliver."

"I had no idea."

"Most people don't, and that's okay. But Daniel gave his life to save a lot of people. Innocent people. I never thought anyone would ever measure up. Then I found Colton." She patted her belly. "Even I was surprised to learn that I could move on and find happiness again. It is possible."

Olivia smiled. "Thanks for sharing that."

"Of course." Elise frowned and shifted behind her. "Listen, you be careful tonight, and I hope you have a good time."

There was one thing that Olivia was certain about.

She would *not* be having a good time.

Especially not if Axel started flirting with every woman in sight like he usually did.

She had no idea why everyone kept calling him a good guy.

He obviously had everyone fooled.

But not Olivia.

She vowed she'd never fall under another man's spell again.

---

AXEL HAD TO GET DRESSED, but first he wanted to study everyone's profile one more time. He needed to be sharp tonight. People's lives depended on it.

He stared at the faces of each of the missing women.

*Their* lives depended on the Blackout team successfully completing this mission also.

Where had these women disappeared to? Were they okay? How many more would vanish before they caught the person responsible?

Because the crimes weren't in the same locations, there was no way to predict where these people would strike next. There was no way to stake out locations and wait for the bad guys to make a move.

In some ways, Axel felt like he was at the mercy of evil men.

That wasn't acceptable.

If the guys with Oasis were somehow behind this, they needed to be stopped. He hoped that by being at the party tonight, some answers would come to light.

His mind went back to Olivia again. He wished she didn't have to be a part of this. Things could turn ugly.

Yet she had volunteered to be involved. Olivia had wanted to see justice served to whoever was behind what was going on. Axel didn't know what exactly had given her that motivation, but it was clearly there.

"We have a dead body."

Axel looked up as Colton stepped into his office.

"What?" Certainly he hadn't heard him correctly.

"One of the women who was missing . . . she turned up. Dead."

## CHAPTER FOURTEEN

"WHO?" Axel asked.

"Lexi Turlington," Colton said.

Axel remembered the facts about her. Twenty-six years old. Accountant. From Northern Virginia.

"Where was she found?" Axel shifted, anxious for more information.

"Her body was found in some woods outside a neighborhood in the DC area."

Axel shook his head as he processed that update. It wasn't what he'd wanted to hear. He'd wanted to find these women before they were hurt.

Failure wasn't acceptable—but failing was precisely what had just happened.

"Anything else?" he asked.

Colton grimaced. "It wasn't good. Her body was . . .

let's just say whoever abducted her didn't show any mercy."

Axel's jaw tightened as he frowned. "I'm sorry to hear that. Were there any clues left, at least?"

"The FBI is investigating. I have a friend who's a contact, and I'm hoping he'll give me any updates. But, as far as we know now, no."

"And no one saw anything?"

Colton shook his head.

Axel frowned and leaned back in his chair. "I've been thinking about tonight . . ."

"About Olivia?"

Axel nodded. "She fits the profile of the women who've gone missing."

"She does. She's professional. Pretty. Single."

And that was precisely what was bothering him. "I'm not sure this is a good idea."

"You said she's going with or without you, right?"

"That's right."

"Then we better make sure you're with her."

---

AS OLIVIA STEPPED into the hallway, Axel's eyes widened, and he let out a low whistle.

"This is one way to make your ex regret his choices," he murmured. "At least, that's how I see it going down."

She wanted to make a snarky remark about that cheesy line about things going down.

But she couldn't.

Instead, Olivia swallowed hard as she stared at Axel.

He'd cleaned up nicely also.

He wore khaki pants with a sky-blue T-shirt that showed off the smooth muscles on his arms and chest. The shirt matched his eyes, which already looked bright below his dark hair.

And this was why so many women fawned over this guy.

If he wasn't a Navy SEAL, he could have been a model.

Olivia forced herself to look away. The last thing she wanted was to admire anything about this man. She knew that sounded crazy, but she needed to keep her distance. Axel seemed to cast his spell on everyone he encountered.

But not Olivia. She wouldn't make that mistake again.

Axel stepped closer and grabbed her hand. She attempted to pull back as fire shot through her at his touch.

But he didn't let go.

That's when she realized he was sliding an engagement ring onto her finger.

She sucked in a breath and stared at the princess-cut diamond set in platinum with six smaller stones surrounding it.

It was breathtaking—and it actually fit.

"Where did you get this?" she asked. "Is it cubic zirconia?"

"No, it's real." He shrugged. "It's not important where it came from."

Olivia begged to differ. There was most *definitely* an important story behind this. But she didn't know him well enough to ask.

Instead, he extended the crook of his arm to her. "Are you ready to go?"

She thought about seeing Tristan again and frowned. She'd probably never be ready for this. But she had no choice but to proceed at this point.

Instead, she'd keep her chin up and make it clear to Tristan that he meant nothing to her anymore. He'd taken someone once so hopeful about love and about the future and turned her into a pessimist.

Olivia nodded as she remembered Axel's question. "Let's get this over with."

## CHAPTER FIFTEEN

AXEL HADN'T EXPECTED his reaction to Olivia.

He'd been around plenty of beautiful ladies in his time. But she really had transformed from a pretty waitress into a beautiful, cultured woman.

Nor had he expected the reaction he felt when he slid that engagement ring on her finger.

Memories of when he'd proposed to Mandy filled his mind, but he shoved them away.

It wasn't the time or the place to dive into those.

If Axel had his way, he'd never relive those memories again. The good times had flipped on their heads and become the worst times, the most painful recollections.

A few minutes later, Axel and Olivia headed down the road in her dark blue sedan. He would have rather taken his motorcycle, but he'd have to save that for another day—a day when Olivia wasn't wearing that dress.

They pulled up to the sprawling three-story house where the retreat was taking place, and Axel put the car in Park. This was one of the oceanfront mansions that had been built here on the island. They hadn't existed here when he was a child. Back then, Lantern Beach had been primarily made up of small beach cottages and fishing cabins.

Things had changed so much.

This place probably had fifteen bedrooms, which made it perfect for an event like this. It was made for large gatherings, and he was sure no expense had been spared inside.

The outside was white with black trim, and the structure stood on stilts, like most homes on this island. The sun was setting, casting a strange mix of gray and muted pastels on the side of the house facing them.

All the lights were on, signaling the party was probably in full swing.

When he looked over, he saw a tremble rake through Olivia.

This was a bad idea, he told himself again. A bad, bad idea.

But if she was going to be here, then she needed someone to watch out for her. That's where he came in.

Axel shifted to face her, needing her to know he

meant what he was about to say. "You sure you're up for this? We can drive away right now. No questions asked. No hard feelings."

She stared at the house in the distance and nodded. "I'm sure I want to do this."

"Understood. I'll try to make it as painless as possible."

"I'd appreciate that." Olivia gave him a look that clearly stated she was dreading this whole charade.

"Are you ready to make our appearance ... dear?"

Her scowl deepened. "Like I said, let's just get this over with."

He hid a smile. He didn't want her here. But, if they were going to work together, at least he could have some fun.

They climbed from her car and headed for the house. She seemed distracted as they climbed the steps to the front door and rang the bell.

A moment later, Rocco answered. With his tux, he looked like the perfect server. Not even a glimmer of recognition filled his gaze as he addressed them.

"Welcome to Oasis Management Systems." He glanced at Olivia. "You must be Olivia. I was told to expect you. Come on in."

As they stepped inside, Axel reached for Olivia's hand. If they acted as cold and stiff to each other as they were acting now, no one would ever believe they were engaged. Olivia was going to have to loosen up.

He wondered if Olivia had thought that one through—if she'd considered the fact she might have to act affectionate.

Based on the way she stiffened when his hand touched hers, probably not.

Before he could say anything to her about it, someone appeared on the stairway in front of them.

Tristan.

Axel tried not to scowl.

Then he braced himself for whatever this man was about to say or do.

---

OLIVIA SQUEEZED Axel's hand a little harder as Tristan stopped in front of them.

Axel seemed to sense her nerves and pulled her even closer.

As he did, Olivia felt herself practically bending into his touch. Something about him screamed "protective," and Olivia hadn't realized how desperately she'd craved his protection.

Craved it? Yes. She wanted more of it.

But she couldn't allow her thoughts to go there. This was simply an arrangement. She needed to remember that Axel was the same flirtatious womanizer she'd seen at The Crazy Chefette. He could act like

Casanova as much as he wanted now, but that's all it was—an act.

Tristan's gaze traveled from Olivia to Axel.

"Glad you made it." But Tristan's voice sounded falsely saccharine.

Tristan's gaze slid between them again, and, for a moment Olivia feared for Axel. Then she remembered the way he'd handled himself yesterday. She needed to believe Axel would still be able to handle himself through whatever happened this evening.

"I told my dad that you were coming." Tristan's laser-beam-like gaze fastened on Olivia. "I'm glad you didn't let me down."

Olivia felt the anger rising in her. The man was so presumptuous. He made some kind of primal rage stir inside her—and she didn't like that feeling. In fact, it made her resent Tristan even more.

Axel bristled and shoved his shoulder in front of hers, placing himself between Olivia and Tristan.

"I'm only here to make sure you don't try to lay a hand on my fiancée again." Axel's voice hardened with each word as he made himself very clear to Tristan.

Olivia held her breath, not expecting those words to come from Axel's lips. Then she realized what he was doing.

It wouldn't be believable if Axel acted like he came here with no qualms after what happened behind The

Crazy Chefette last night. The issue needed to be addressed in order to seem real.

Tristan gazed at him coolly. "I'm sorry I let things get the best of me. It won't happen again."

Axel kept his gaze narrow. "No, it won't."

The two stared at each other a moment until finally Tristan nodded toward the stairs. "Why don't you guys come on in? I'll find my dad for you."

Still gripping Axel's hand, Olivia followed Tristan up two flights of stairs to the third floor. At the top, the main living area stretched in front of them. Various people mingled there, sipping drinks and munching on appetizers as a guitarist played in the background.

Olivia glanced at the driftwood-colored wooden floors, the white cabinets, the marble countertops. A large deck jutted from three sets of patio doors against one wall. On the other side of that was the ocean. The mighty Atlantic.

The place was gorgeous, and Olivia couldn't even imagine what a place like this would run for a week.

"I say we buy this for our first home," Axel muttered. "Think we can manage the mortgage payments on it?"

She laughed despite herself. "Absolutely."

"We like it here." Tristan joined them and stared out at the water. "Can I get you something to drink?"

"Water sounds great." Olivia's voice sounded tense

to her own ears, and she kept catching herself rubbing the bruise on her arm. She had to stop doing that.

She'd added more makeup to cover the area, but if she kept touching it she might reveal the damage. She could imagine Axel's response.

And the ensuing tension that would cause.

This party couldn't be over soon enough.

"Water for me too," Axel added.

"Very well." Tristan headed into the kitchen.

Olivia exchanged a glance with Axel. Being here now . . . it suddenly felt like a very bad idea. Why did she ever think she could pull this off? That she could somehow find a way to help nail Tristan for whatever he'd done?

She should have asked more questions. She shouldn't have volunteered so easily.

But she'd seen the opportunity and had seized it. Being here made her feel like she had some of her power back—power that Tristan had stripped from her.

Axel stepped closer, releasing her hand and gently touching her waist as he leaned in. His breath brushed across her ear as he said, "Try to relax. You look tense."

Feeling him so close did nothing to help that.

Especially when she smelled his leathery aftershave.

She wasn't supposed to like the scent.

But she did.

She swallowed hard and glanced around, willing herself not to lean closer for another whiff.

"Long time, no see," a deep voice said behind her.

Olivia swirled at the familiar voice.

When she saw the man standing there, her legs began to tremble.

Leo Bennett? What was he doing here?

## CHAPTER SIXTEEN

AXEL BRISTLED when he saw the large man staring at Olivia with interest in his eyes.

He recognized him from the photos he'd studied earlier.

Leo Bennett, Stan Bennett's older son.

The one poised to take over the company one day.

Or was that Tristan?

It wasn't clear.

"Leo..." Olivia muttered, instinctively taking a step back. "I wasn't expecting to see you here."

The man sized up Axel before he turned back to Olivia. "You're looking more beautiful than ever."

He took her hand and kissed the top, his lips lingering over her fingers a little too long.

Despite the fact that they weren't even really engaged, Axel felt the tension ripple through him.

The man held onto Olivia's hand a moment longer and stared at the ring there. "Engaged?"

"Yes." Olivia's voice trembled as she pulled her hand away and turned to Axel. "Leo, this is my fiancé, Axel Hendrix. Axel, Leo Bennett."

The man openly studied Axel, not bothering to hide his scrutiny. "You're a lucky man."

Axel slipped an arm around Olivia's waist. "You don't have to tell me. I know a good thing when I see it."

Axel glanced at Olivia and winked.

As he did, Olivia's cheeks reddened.

She was going to have to watch that telltale reaction or their whole cover was going to be blown. Axel would mention it to her later.

Olivia turned back to Leo. "How is everything with Oasis?"

"I can't complain. If things stay on track, I'll be taking over when my father retires next year."

"What about Tristan?"

Leo smirked. "He'll be lucky if he's left anything in the will."

"I see." Olivia's throat looked strained, like she couldn't swallow, as she stared at the man.

"You recognize most of the people here anymore?" Leo scanned the crowd.

"I can't say I do." She nodded to a tall man with dark hair in the distance. "Who is he?"

"Him? Mitch Abrams, the new VP of operations."

"When did he start?"

Leo shrugged. "Six months ago. Can't say he's really done much. He's always on the phone or taking personal time."

Six months? Taking time off? Axel stored that information away.

Because whoever had abducted those women would most likely need to be out of the office quite a bit.

Someone across the room called Leo away, but the man turned back to Olivia first. "It was nice to see you. I'd love to catch up sometime."

There was no way Axel wanted that to happen. This guy . . . he screamed trouble. This whole company did, for that matter.

Olivia said nothing, just offered a polite smile and nod as the man walked away.

"Why did you turn five shades whiter when you saw him?" Axel leaned in toward Olivia as he asked the question. "And make sure you let out a little giggle so we don't look like we're undercover but like we're in love."

She let out a laugh, but it sounded forced. Then, through clenched teeth, she said, "You think Tristan's bad? Leo is like Tristan only tripled. Tristan responds out of emotion. Leo . . . he's calculated. He knows what he wants, and he doesn't let anything get in the way of it."

Axel followed the man across the room with his gaze. It sounded like Leo was someone they needed to put on their watch list.

Just then, Tristan appeared with their water.

"Sorry I took so long." Tristan handed over the glasses and smoothed the edge of his black golf shirt. "I saw you ran into Leo."

Axel noticed Tristan's eyes darken when he said his brother's name. Obviously, a history stood between them.

"Yes, I haven't seen him in quite a while." Olivia's voice sounded stiff as she said the words. "And what about your father? Where is he?"

"He'll be here soon."

Axel watched the way a vein popped out in Tristan's neck. This conversation was causing the man's anger and adrenaline to rise. He made a mental note of that fact.

Axel raised his glass. "If you don't mind, I'm going to steal Olivia away so we can go outside and catch a glimpse of the ocean together."

Tristan frowned but nodded. "Of course. I'll be around. Don't worry. We can talk more later."

Axel was sure that was the case. But right now he sensed that Olivia needed a little breathing room.

And that was exactly what he wanted to give her.

OLIVIA COULDN'T BREATHE. Thank goodness, Axel had suggested going outside. Maybe some fresh air would fix this.

Her insides felt like they were tangled up in knots.

She was never going to pull this off if she continued to feel this jittery.

Axel led her to the balcony, his hand still on her back. She was sure he didn't realize how his touch made all her nerve endings feel jumpy and alive.

Which was the last thing Olivia wanted.

He leaned close enough that nobody else could hear. "Are you okay?"

The tender way he said the words almost made Olivia believe that he cared. Then she reminded herself they were "undercover" as Axel had called it earlier. All this was just an act.

She inadvertently rubbed her bruise again. "Leo... he's always frightened me. Maybe you're right. Maybe I shouldn't have come."

"It's not too late to abort this mission. You could feign a sickness."

That idea was tempting. But Olivia had come here to make a good impression in front of Tristan's dad.

If she didn't, then Tristan was going to share her secret with everybody. She couldn't let him do that.

Besides, she wanted to help bring the man down. The whole family was corrupt.

Maybe not Stan.

Or did she only think that because the man had always been kind to her?

Everything seemed hazy in her mind, and Olivia felt uncertain about every aspect of this. Just what were the Bennetts up to? She needed to know more details.

But right now wasn't the time to ask.

"The ocean sure is pretty, isn't it?" Axel stared out at the beach in front of them.

It was a welcome change of subject. "It sure is. I could stare at it all day."

"What brought you to this area, Olivia?"

As soon as Axel asked that question, any of the peace Olivia had felt ran away like it was being chased.

"I just needed a change." She wanted to switch the subject from herself as quickly as possible. "You?"

"I actually grew up here in Lantern Beach."

Surprise rushed through her. She hadn't expected that. He seemed more like the city type. "Oh, really?"

"Really. I joined the military as soon as I graduated from high school, and I never came back until recently."

"Does your family still live here?"

His jaw tightened. "No, not anymore. It was just me and my mom for a long time. She ended up getting remarried and moved to New Mexico."

Olivia glanced up at him. "New Mexico?"

"That's right. She met somebody online, and they fell in love. I'm really happy for her. Her marriage to my dad wasn't all that great, so she deserves to be with somebody who treats her well."

The depth of caring in his voice made something warm grow inside her.

Maybe there was more to Axel Hendrix than she'd thought.

Maybe.

# CHAPTER SEVENTEEN

OLIVIA LICKED her lips and looked back toward the ocean.

She would stay out here for a little bit longer. Then she needed to find Tristan's dad and get that whole meet and greet over with.

After a few moments of quiet, Axel turned to watch the people inside. "You recognize any of them?"

He nodded toward the house.

Olivia turned and perused the guests. "There's Clive Cleveland standing off to the side. He's Stan's right-hand man. He's uptight—then again, you have to be to do the job."

Clive was small and thin with a receding hairline, quick motions, and even quicker words. He defined Type A.

"Anyone else?"

She nodded to a woman with wedged blonde hair and a tight dress. "That's Miranda Philips. She's the head of marketing."

Olivia frowned as she said the words.

"Bad blood between the two of you?"

Olivia shrugged. "Let's just say she's not my favorite person. She looks out for one person—herself."

Everyone in the office had admired Miranda for her go get 'em attitude and no-holds-barred style of leadership. But the woman had been so ambitious that she'd made it clear she'd trample over anyone who got in her way.

At that thought, Olivia saw Tristan approaching again.

What now? Couldn't he give them a minute alone? But the man had always been the jealous type.

He could cheat on Olivia all he wanted, but the moment he thought Olivia wasn't being faithful . . . he went ballistic.

She cringed at the memories.

"Tell me," Axel started. "Who's the genius behind this company? The one who developed the software?"

Tristan paused in front of them and frowned. "My father."

"He's still the one in the driver's seat, so to speak?" Axel continued.

"That's right. He was brilliant before his time.

People think the tech business is a young man's world, but my father does it all. He's very hands on."

"Stan is an amazing man," Olivia added.

"When's the date?" Tristan asked.

Olivia blinked. "What date?"

She had no idea what he was talking about.

A new gleam entered Tristan's gaze as he nodded at her hand. "Your wedding date."

The air left her lungs. Of course. How could she have forgotten?

She swallowed hard.

Had she just blown her cover?

---

AXEL WAITED to see what Tristan might say next.

He needed to do damage control—and fast.

"October," Axel said. "We're getting married in October."

Olivia let out a nervous laugh. "Of course. I don't know where my mind was."

Tristan's eyes narrowed. "I thought you always wanted a summer wedding."

"That was you, not me." Her voice sounded terse.

This guy was getting under her skin, wasn't he?

"So . . . how did you two meet?" Tristan started, a pointed tone to his voice.

Axel could sense the anxiety stirring in Olivia. The

two of them had come up with a cover story earlier. But the key was making it believable.

"Why don't you tell him?" Axel said.

Her cheeks reddened. "It was really a meeting to remember. I was out riding my bike on the boardwalk after I'd moved to Lantern Beach. I hit a stick and fell."

"She was quite the sight," Axel added. "I happened to be there to help her up."

"Sounds like you always show up in the nick of time." Tristan scowled.

"I do." Axel's voice hardened. "It was like love at first sight. She was the most beautiful woman I'd ever seen, and I knew I'd be a fool to ever let her go. What can I say? That's how it all went down."

Axel pulled Olivia closer, despite how stiff she felt.

She let out a breath before giggling and resting her hand on Axel's chest. "Oh, you. Stop!"

Tristan narrowed his eyes in scrutiny before turning back to Axel. "Have you always lived here?"

He was really giving him the third degree, wasn't he? Axel knew he had to roll with it—for now.

"I grew up on the island but then joined the military," he said. "I only came back here four months ago."

Tristan grunted. "What do you do?"

"I work from home. For a health insurance company. Pretty boring stuff, really."

"Sounds like it." Tristan casually rested his hands

in his pockets as if their meeting was a casual, everyday occurrence.

Axel's gaze followed Mitch Abrams as the man put his phone to his ear. He glanced around—suspiciously—before creeping toward the door.

Axel sucked in a breath, knowing he had to make a quick choice.

Follow him or stay with Olivia?

## CHAPTER EIGHTEEN

"OLIVIA . . . can I talk to you a minute?" Tristan asked.

Talking to Tristan was the last thing Olivia wanted. But the look in his eyes . . . it was pure malice and threat.

Axel turned toward Tristan with a glare. Yet his motions seemed stiffer than before, and he kept glancing toward the house.

Did he know something that she didn't?

"Anything you have to say to her, you can say in front of me," Axel growled.

As expected, Tristan's gaze darkened. "It's a private conversation. I'm sure Olivia gets *the picture*."

The picture?

Her breath caught. She knew exactly what Tristan was getting at. His words were a subtle threat that he could spill her secret.

That he would share the picture he had of her . . . the one that presented her in a terrible light.

She had no choice but to chat with Tristan. If she didn't . . . there was no way Axel would want to continue their charade. Not if he knew . . .

Olivia turned to her fake fiancé. "It'll be fine. Just for a minute."

Axel's jaw tightened, and she wasn't sure he was going to go for it.

"It sounds like a bad idea."

"I just need to show her something," Tristan said. "I won't take her away from you for long. Scout's honor."

As if Tristan had ever been a scout . . .

Axel's gaze remained hard but he finally nodded. "It's Olivia's choice."

Relief filled her as she nodded. "I'll be right back."

---

AXEL'S protective instincts told him not to let Olivia go.

But she seemed willing. Surprisingly willing.

How could he stop her without making a scene?

He knew the answer. He couldn't.

Besides, he wanted to know what was going on with Mitch. The more he thought about it, the more he realized this man's timeline fit with the crimes.

"Don't go far, sweetie." Axel offered a quick smile.

But he didn't like this.

He only hoped that Tristan didn't try to take her anywhere out of sight.

Olivia nodded.

Axel expected her to look more nervous. But she seemed surprisingly calm as she walked back inside with Tristan.

Either she was great at doing this type of thing... or she had ulterior motives.

Could she be trusted?

He wanted to believe she could. But he needed to be on guard.

Axel wandered back into the living room as well. As Tristan and Olivia disappeared down the hall together, tension stretched through his body.

Axel was only giving them five minutes. Then he was going in.

"Would you like another glass of water?"

Axel looked up as Rocco approached him. "As a matter of fact, I would."

He exchanged his old glass for a new one.

"I need to go follow Mitch Abrams," Axel whispered. "Olivia just went to talk with Tristan."

"Is that a good idea?"

"Probably not. But I couldn't stop her."

"I'll keep my eyes open for trouble."

"Thanks."

Axel slipped to the other side of the house.

A stairway stretched in front of him.

Mitch must have gone this way.

He glanced around to make sure no one was watching before heading down the stairs.

As soon as he reached the bottom floor, he heard a voice ringing out.

Was that Mitch?

Axel remained around the corner and listened.

"I have a shipment coming, but it's been delayed," he said. "I can assure you, we'll have what we need in time."

Were the abducted women the shipment he was talking about?

Axel's breath caught.

Before he could head back up the stairs, Mitch appeared in front of him.

The man shoved the phone back into his pocket as he stared at Axel.

Axel put on his most friendly smile. "Bathroom?"

Mitch scowled. "I'd use the one upstairs if I were you."

Axel nodded. "I'll do that. Thanks."

He headed back up the stairs.

It was time to find Olivia anyway.

The five minutes were up.

## CHAPTER NINETEEN

TRISTAN LED Olivia into a dimly lit bedroom and shut the door behind him.

As he did, a shiver ran through her.

The next instant, he backed her into the wall and leered at her.

Standing close.

Too close.

*Dangerously* close.

Close enough to wrap a hand around her neck if he wanted to.

Just what was Tristan going to do to her in here? Did she really want to find out?

Olivia should have stayed with Axel. Should have feigned an excuse. Should have listened to the silent warnings Axel shot her with his gaze.

Tristan stepped close enough that she felt his body heat. He glanced down at her, a lustful look in his eyes.

"I'm glad you came tonight, Olivia."

She kept her gaze even, determined not to let him have any power over her. "I only came because you threatened me."

He reached up and wiped a hair out of her eyes. "You know I've never stopped loving you."

Her panic mixed with something close to disgust, and she held up her hand so he could see her ring—her fantastic, albeit fake—ring. "You know I'm engaged."

Tristan's expression remained stony, almost as if he hadn't heard her. "You don't really love him. I can see it on your face. You're just going through the motions."

Had he really seen that? Had he sensed their relationship wasn't real? Or was he blowing smoke?

"You're wrong." Her voice cracked. "I do love Axel."

"But we had something special." Tristan leaned close enough that Olivia feared he might try to kiss her.

If Tristan decided to try anything . . . she wouldn't be able to get away.

Olivia wanted to cry for help, but the words seemed to die in her throat.

Her lungs tightened as she tried to figure out what to do.

She should have never agreed to come with him.

But she couldn't let him be in control now.

Olivia sucked in a deep breath before locking her gaze with him. "Why did you bring me in here? Where's your dad? Why isn't he here yet? Talking to him was part of the deal."

Tristan shrugged. "Unfortunately, he got called away to do something else tonight."

Olivia's stomach dropped. "What?"

"Sorry. It was all last minute or I would have let you know beforehand."

"Tristan . . ." Olivia didn't believe him. She'd bet any and everything he'd known exactly what was going on. He just wanted another chance to catch her alone.

But why? What did her ex really want from her? To use her "magic touch" with his father? Or did he want her back?

"I needed to see you," he murmured.

She sucked in a breath. Was that really it? Did he want to win back her affection?

No. He was just trying to regain control, she reminded herself.

She needed this man out of her life.

For good.

Preferably with him behind bars.

"How did you end up here?" Olivia asked. "How did this retreat end up being in Lantern Beach of all places?"

Tristan shrugged, a certain smugness entering his

gaze. "They asked my opinion on where the retreat should be held. I thought, why not Lantern Beach?"

The air left her lungs as realization hit her. "You knew I was here, didn't you? That's why you picked this location. It's why you're here now."

Was Tristan the one leaving her those notes? Was he playing some kind of game with her?

He smirked. "What can I say? I would do anything for you."

This was far from over. Tristan wasn't going to give up. Although she had hoped he would really leave her alone as he'd said he would, Olivia suspected he would renege on his word.

Nothing with him was ever that easy.

"What do you want from me?"

"Two things. First, I need you to be my good luck charm. Leo doesn't deserve to take over this company. I do. I need you to convince my father of that."

"And second?"

"Forget about that other guy. You need to be with me."

"Tristan—"

"I won't take no for an answer."

When Olivia looked into his eyes, she knew that he was telling the truth.

She'd tangled herself in this web, and now she had no idea how she was going to get out of it . . . at least, get out of it in one piece.

OLIVIA STILL WASN'T BACK in the living room yet.

Axel needed to find her.

Now.

He stormed down the hallway. He knew exactly which room they'd gone into.

When he reached the door, he threw it open and saw Tristan standing in front of Olivia, pressing her against the wall.

Another surge of anger ripped through him.

Axel pulled Olivia away from the man and pushed her behind him. His muscles bristled as adrenaline pumped through him.

He glared at Tristan. "Your talk is over."

Tristan glared back. "I wouldn't be so sure about that, buddy. This is between Olivia and me."

"I thought you were showing her something," Axel muttered.

Tristan stepped back and straightened. "I was."

Axel waited to hear what that might be.

The man grabbed a piece of paper from a nightstand. "It's a job offer. I want her back at Oasis. We should have never let her go."

"You couldn't have made that offer in front of me?"

"I didn't think you would appreciate the idea of me taking her off this island." He smirked.

Guys like this . . . they made Axel want to teach them a lesson.

But there were better ways than fighting.

Axel mostly wanted to see this guy behind bars.

He gathered all his self-control before muttering, "That will be the last time that you talk to my fiancée in private."

Tristan smirked again. "We'll see about that."

Axel felt his hands fist at his side. He was about to retort when another figure stepped into the room.

Leo.

If Axel started something now, chaos would break out at the house.

He didn't want that to happen, for more than one reason.

But these guys were creeps. They didn't need to be at large out in the world.

That was a problem for another time.

Right now, Olivia's safety was priority.

"We're getting out of here." Axel took Olivia's hand. "You two have a nice day."

He wasn't sure if Leo was going to move out of his way or not. But he finally did. Axel kept Olivia's hand in his as he led her down the hallway. He didn't stop until they were out the front door.

He wanted to pause on the front deck and talk to her.

But that wouldn't be wise.

Instead, he led her to her car and paused there. No one else was around.

Axel knew he should let her hand go. That probably nobody else was watching and they could drop their act.

But he didn't want to do that. He somehow still felt himself holding on as he turned toward Olivia. "Did he hurt you?"

"Tristan isn't going to give up." Her voice sounded thin, almost fragile. "I don't know how far he'll take things, but this fake engagement can't go on anymore. If Tristan gets it into his mind to kill you, that's exactly what he is going to do."

She was panicking, wasn't she? She was worried about Axel, of all people. She needed to worry about herself right now. He could take care of himself.

"Tristan's not going to kill me," Axel assured her. "I can handle myself."

"You don't know Tristan. He doesn't play fair. He's more of the sneaky type. And I'll never forgive myself if something happens to you because of me."

"Olivia . . ." Gone was the feisty woman Axel had originally met. This situation had flipped things upside down for her.

As she stood in front of him now, trembles captured her limbs.

He wasn't sure how it happened. If he leaned toward her, or if Olivia leaned toward him. Either way,

Axel wrapped his arms around her, wishing he could do something else to offer Olivia comfort. That conversation had obviously shaken her up—and for good reason.

These guys weren't to be messed with.

One thing was certain: bringing Olivia into this had been a huge mistake.

That fact was only confirmed when Axel heard a footstep beside them.

## CHAPTER TWENTY

OLIVIA GASPED and stepped closer to Axel.

Who was here?

The same person sending her those notes? Whom she could feel watching her?

A man stepped out of the shadows.

As his face came into focus, Olivia released her breath and eased away from Axel.

"Stan . . ." She shook her head. "I thought you were gone."

"Olivia Rollins! I didn't mean to scare you. I'm staying next door and decided to walk over. That's when I saw you standing here."

Though both of his sons were tall and muscular, Stan Bennett stood at a modest five foot eight and was of an average build. He had thick salt-and-pepper hair that he combed up away from his face. It stood at least two inches high, and she'd often wondered if he did that to make himself look taller. His skin was always unusually tan and his teeth startling white.

Stan shook his head as he observed her. "It's been too long since I've seen my lucky charm!"

That's what he always called Olivia. He said good things happened when she was around.

He pulled her into a hug, and then stepped back, still observing her. "Tristan said you were in town. You look fantastic. You always do."

"Thank you."

Stan's gaze shifted to Axel. "And who is this with you?"

"Stan, this is Axel . . . my fiancé . . ." Olivia swallowed hard, guilt flooding her. She hated lying—especially to someone who seemed to admire her.

"Your fiancé?" His eyes widened. "I wasn't expecting that. To be honest, I was still hoping you and Tristan would get back together. You were good for him."

She offered an apologetic shrug. "Your son and I . . . we're over."

Stan frowned. "I know. I know. But a man can hope, right? This new guy better be treating you right."

Funny he'd said that since his own son had never treated her right. But she kept her mouth shut.

"Yes, sir." Axel slipped his arm around her waist.

Stan's gaze went from Axel back to Olivia. "I'm

sorry I missed you tonight. How about we have dinner tomorrow? You can bring Axel along."

Olivia glanced up at Axel, trying to gage his reaction.

Before she could figure it out, she blurted, "We'd love to."

Love to? Did she really want to do this? At least if Axel was by her side, she wouldn't feel so exposed. Plus, it seemed like the perfect opportunity to find out more information.

"Perfect."

They exchanged numbers, and Stan promised to text the details.

Then they said goodbye.

Olivia let out a breath as he disappeared from sight, and she turned to Axel.

"I hope you're okay with dinner?" she asked. "You don't have to do this."

"I want to. It will be a good opportunity to find out more about the company. But we can cancel if it makes you uncomfortable."

She thought about it a moment before shaking her head. "No, it will be fine. I want to do whatever I can to stop Tristan."

Axel stared at her another moment before nodding. "Okay then. Great. Now, let's get you home. It's been a long night."

Getting home sounded perfect.

OLIVIA STARED out the window as they headed down the road. Darkness surrounded them, and, sadly, it was beginning to match the darkness she felt in her soul.

Not that she was letting herself become one of the bad guys.

It was just that life had worn her down and sometimes she found herself giving in to despair.

Like right now.

What would it take to stop Tristan?

She felt like nothing could stop him.

And now she'd involved somebody else.

"Stan seems to like you a lot," Axel said as he gripped the wheel.

Olivia frowned as she remembered their history. "He does. I, um . . . this is going to sound strange, but . . . I saved his life once."

"What?"

She nodded as that day flooded back into her mind. "One day, as I was about to walk into the office, Stan pulled up to the front of the building in his car. As the driver let him out, another vehicle lost control as it came down the road. I saw the car careening toward Stan, and I pushed him out of the way. If I hadn't . . ."

"He would have died," Axel finished.

"Or been seriously injured. After that, I was like his

best friend. Then when I started dating Tristan... Stan welcomed me with open arms. I hope he's not guilty in any of this."

"Do you think he is?"

Olivia thought about it a moment before shrugging. "I don't know. He has a big personality, and he hates it when people aren't loyal to him. He got mad at Tristan and cut him out of the company for a while. He's a very black-and-white type of guy. There's no in-between."

"Good to know."

Olivia felt something change in the air and glanced at Axel. His gaze tightened as he stared at the road ahead before glancing in the rearview mirror.

Something was different.

What was going on?

Olivia glanced behind her and saw headlights there.

"I think we're being followed," he said.

"Who would be following us?"

"I have no idea who it could be or what they're planning."

Olivia frowned. "They're so far away. That's a good sign, right?"

"It beats being rammed by another vehicle. That's for sure."

"Have you been rammed by another vehicle? Never

mind. I don't want to know." She gripped the armrest beside her. "What are we going to do?"

"I can't let them follow us. They might already know where you live. But I'm not going to lead them there."

"Tristan was at my house last night. He knows where I live."

"What if Tristan isn't the bad guy here?"

Her throat tightened. The thought of there being more than one bad guy didn't bring her any comfort. Then again, it probably took a network of people to pull off an identity theft operation.

She glanced behind her again and saw that the headlights were still there.

The problem was that in a place like Lantern Beach, there weren't that many places to go.

A single stretch of highway ran down the center of the narrow island. Various streets jutted out from it, but most of them were dead ends.

That didn't give them many choices as far as getting away.

Suddenly, Axel jerked the wheel to the right.

Olivia closed her eyes, not sure what to expect next.

But she prayed they'd survive this.

AXEL GRIPPED THE WHEEL, not liking what he saw behind him. Was this the same person who'd run him off the road last night? Had they come back to finish what they started?

Even though the other driver was staying a decent distance back, Axel felt certain they were being followed.

Which could lead to more trouble.

What he wasn't sure about was why.

Most likely, somebody simply wanted to send a message.

But Axel wasn't in the mood for games.

He turned into a school parking lot and drove toward the back of the building.

"What are you doing?" Olivia gripped the arm rest still, her voice rising in pitch.

"Trying to get these guys off our tail."

"I see." Her voice cracked.

Axel couldn't blame her. Anybody in this situation would be nervous.

Moving quickly, he drove behind the school building before circling back around near the bus ramp.

He cut his lights, then parked behind a dumpster.

He wanted to see if this person would be brazen enough to come after him here.

Hopefully, the driver would just continue past.

But Axel needed to be ready for anything.

He waited, readying himself to act.

A moment later, headlights came from around the corner behind him.

He frowned.

It looked like these guys hadn't given up after all.

## CHAPTER TWENTY-ONE

OLIVIA'S HEART pounded into her chest.

Whoever had followed them had found them. Was there even time for her and Axel to get away now? What would the driver of that car do if he managed to get his hands on them?

Axel put the car into Drive.

As he did, lights flashed behind them.

Police lights.

"Do you think it's really the cops?" Olivia rushed. "What if it's only someone pretending to be law enforcement?"

Maybe she watched a lot of crime shows on TV. Still, it would benefit them to be careful. Being too trusting seemed like the formula for getting killed.

"I don't know," Axel said. "But we're going to wait right here until we know for sure. Don't make any sudden moves and follow my lead. If things go south, just know that I've got your back."

Olivia could hardly breathe as she waited to see what would happen next.

From where she sat, she saw someone climb from the vehicle behind her. But because of the lights, everything seemed shadowed. She couldn't make out enough details.

*Please, Lord. I'm not ready to die. Please.*

A moment later, Axel lowered his window.

A friendly face appeared there.

Police Chief Cassidy Chambers. The woman was friends with Lisa and often came into the restaurant. She'd always seemed kind and fair—but also like someone who you didn't want to get on her bad side.

"Axel?" Cassidy questioned.

Axel waved his hand in the air. "It's me."

Cassidy's gaze shot to the passenger seat. "Olivia?"

Olivia felt her muscles loosen as she smiled at the police chief. "Hi, Chief."

"I saw someone pull behind the school building, and I wanted to make sure everything was on the up and up. You guys okay?"

"We're fine." Axel shrugged, looking as casual as ever. "Just coming back from a party."

"And you took a detour behind the school?" Cassidy stared at Axel, doubt staining her gaze.

He shrugged. "I was giving Olivia a tour of the

island. I was the quarterback for the school's football team in high school. Nothing like reliving those glory days."

Cassidy tilted her head and squinted even more. It was obvious she didn't buy his story. "The parking lot is closed, I'm sorry to inform you."

"Good to know."

Olivia shook her head beside him. Certainly, Axel was going to mention that they were being followed . . . right?

Olivia was going to have to defer to his experience on this.

A moment later, Cassidy tapped the side of the car door and stepped toward her cruiser.

When she was gone, Axel turned to Olivia, his shoulders seeming more relaxed—not that they'd ever really looked tense. "That was close."

"Why didn't you just tell her the truth?" she asked.

"I'm going to let Colton do that. Cassidy's husband, Ty, helped start Blackout. I'd rather Colton decides how much to say about this."

She supposed that made sense. "Now, what about the car that was following us?"

"I'll continue to keep my eyes open for them. In the meantime, let's get you home. You've had a long day."

Olivia couldn't argue with that.

And it didn't look like things would be calmer any time soon.

AXEL GLANCED AROUND as he walked Olivia up to her apartment.

Though he'd been here earlier, he hadn't been paying much attention.

Now, his senses were on high alert.

The upstairs neighbor blared music. That was annoying within itself. But the tunes also concealed any telltale sounds around them.

It wasn't that the apartment complex was bad. It simply housed vagabonds in this area. Surfers brought their own sets of trouble with them. Axel would know.

That had been him in high school—only he'd been able to stay at home with his mom. But he knew plenty about the type because he'd been one. Thankfully, he'd stayed away from drugs that were so prevalent in the culture. That had been mostly his mom's influence on him.

After fumbling with the lock for a moment, Olivia finally opened her door and turned toward him. "Listen, I know this was a strange arrangement. But thank you for everything tonight."

Axel nodded behind her. "Not to be forward, but can I come in?"

She stared at him a moment as if questioning her options.

"If anyone's watching, they'll think it's weird that I

didn't," Axel explained. "Especially since I'm your fiancé. Plus, I'd like to check things out."

Her expression seemed to soften. "Good point. Come on in. No funny business."

"Funny business? Me?"

"I see how you are with women, and I just want to let you know that I will *not* be falling under your spell."

"And I just want to let you know that I absolutely, positively do *not* have any spells I cast on people."

Olivia almost snorted. "You could have fooled me."

Axel stepped in behind her and closed the door. "You've been keeping an eye on me?"

"It's more like I can't help but notice the monstrosity of women following you around at The Crazy Chefette. Other places too, I'm sure."

He shrugged again. "They're just being friendly."

She rolled her eyes. "I'm sure that's what they're doing."

"Glad to see I convinced you."

She nodded toward the couch in the living room. "Would you like to sit for a minute? I can get you something to drink, though I don't have a lot. Room temperature water or ice water. What's your pleasure?"

"Room temperature water sounds great." After checking out the rest of her place, he made himself comfortable on the couch.

As he did, he glanced around. This wasn't how Axel had expected Olivia's place to be decorated. The apartment looked rather bland. Axel would bet this furniture had come with the place. That made the most sense.

He had to admit that he was curious to see a different side of her than the one he'd observed at the restaurant.

Sure, he had noticed Olivia before. Who wouldn't? The woman was beautiful. She always had a friendly smile for customers and seemed good at exchanging chitchat.

With everyone except him, he'd noticed.

Did she always avoid his table? Or was that just a coincidence?

Axel knew what his guess was.

As Olivia grabbed the water, he quickly texted Rocco about what had happened. Rocco immediately responded.

Tristan and Leo had been at the party all night.

Neither of them had been the ones in that car following them.

He frowned.

So who had it been?

Olivia returned with a bottle of water and handed it to him before sitting on the other end of the couch.

She slipped off her sandals and pulled her legs beneath her as she turned toward him. "What do we do now?"

"I don't know. Drink water. Talk."

She threw a pillow at him. "I mean, after this charade we pulled off tonight."

He threw the pillow back at her. "Oh, that. We were quite the actors."

"People might have even thought we were in love."

He raised his eyebrows. "Hard to imagine, huh?"

She almost snorted as she tossed the pillow back at him. "Believe someone would be in love with you? Absolutely."

"Oh... you had to go there." Axel shook his head, a grin stretched across his face.

The next instant, Olivia sobered. "Listen, I'm sorry about agreeing to dinner with Tristan's father. I should have said no."

Axel begged to differ. His only concern was Olivia. "Dinner with him will be perfect. He's the exact guy I need to talk to. I just wish that you didn't have to be there."

"Well, it's kind of like I come with the territory." She frowned.

Axel's thoughts raced as he tried to think through the logistics of the situation. "That means we're also going to need to keep up this charade while we're out and about in town. If one of these guys catches us, and people find out that we're not engaged... I don't like the position that's going to put you in. Especially now that I've seen Tristan and his brother in action."

Olivia shuddered and grabbed the pillow she'd

thrown at him only moments earlier. This time, she hugged the navy-blue poof to her chest. "What a nightmare."

Again Axel was reminded of everything she'd been through—and everything that was yet to come. If he could think of a way to do this without her, he'd jump on the opportunity. But there was no other way.

Maybe he simply needed to drive home the seriousness of the situation. "Olivia . . . I don't think you realize just how dangerous these guys are."

She nibbled on her bottom lip before saying, "I guess I don't. But I know I want to bring them down. I can't sit idly by and do nothing. Not if I can help."

Axel stared at her another moment.

He appreciated her spirit and determination. The woman had surprised him in more than one way. She was more than a pretty face. And she definitely wasn't the type who wanted to fall all over him.

There was a part of him that found that very attractive.

But he prayed he could keep Olivia safe.

Because whoever was abducting these women . . . they would stop at nothing to get what they wanted.

## CHAPTER TWENTY-TWO

"CAN I ASK YOU SOMETHING?"

Olivia froze at Axel's question. That was always a set up for when someone was going to ask something nosy.

But Axel had put himself on the line for her, so she couldn't say no.

"Whatcha got?"

"How did you and Tristan meet?"

Her eyes widened. "Oh, that. I actually worked as a marketing consultant for his company for almost a year. We met there, and he pursued me as if winning my heart would be better than closing the biggest deal of his life. Honestly, it was quite flattering at the time."

Axel shifted, his gaze lighting with curiosity. "Wait, you worked for Oasis?"

"I did. That's where I started my career. But when

Tristan and I got engaged, I decided I should work for a different company. It felt weird to be engaged to someone who was officially my boss."

Axel leaned forward, elbows on his legs and his full attention on her. "I'm going to need to get back to the fact you worked for Oasis in a minute. First, how long did the two of you date?"

"Six months. Honestly, that's the perfect amount of time for someone to hide who they really are. Most people can pull something like that off for that amount of time. I saw little cracks here and there, but I brushed them off and assumed he was having a bad day. I didn't really know exactly how much he was hiding."

"I'd say. How long were you engaged?"

"Two months. I broke up with him six months ago. I should have done it right away. Because things went south after we were engaged, and I could see the writing on the wall. I wanted to believe there was still something good inside Tristan, that I hadn't been totally fooled."

"I guess it can happen to the best of us."

She glanced at Axel, studying his expression and wondering about his words. "Have you been there too?"

Axel didn't say anything for a moment. But Olivia noticed his eyes went to the engagement ring on her finger.

He suddenly straightened, his casual demeanor

disappearing. "Actually, we should talk about your time at Oasis."

She nodded slowly, getting the message loud and clear. It was fine for her to talk about her personal life, but Axel had no interest in talking about his own experiences.

His avoidance stung a little. Which surprised her.

But it also reminded her that distance was a good thing, even though Olivia had just broken down a few walls on her end.

She frowned, wishing she could take back what she'd so openly shared. Most likely, she would regret doing so.

But it was too late for that.

Whatever. It was just as well.

She repressed a sigh and said, "What do you need to know?"

---

FOR A MOMENT, Axel contemplated telling Olivia about his marriage. About his heartbreak. About when his wife had left, and how there had been nothing he could do that would win her back.

Now, Mandy was remarried with a child on the way.

But he never talked about that. He never talked about Mandy.

He wanted to keep it that way. To hide his pain and keep it private.

As tempting as the idea was to open up to Olivia and as cozy as she looked as she sat on the couch with a pillow pulled her chest, it was better if they stuck to business.

"Did you see anything suspicious within the company when you worked for Oasis?"

Olivia seemed to think about it a moment before shaking her head. "Not really. I mean, I was the new girl in the office. But I didn't see anything that raised any red flags."

"What about outside of the job? You've been around these guys. Did they ever say anything that made you uncomfortable? That made you wonder if something else was going on?"

She let out a long breath and didn't say anything for a moment. "Stan, Leo, and Tristan were always having private meetings. Mostly with people I'd never seen before and with companies I'd never heard of. It just seemed like the status quo around there. I figured, what did I really know about this kind of thing? Nothing. I know marketing. So that's what I stuck to."

More questions raced through Axel's head. Questions about how somebody who had worked in marketing was now working as a waitress. It just wasn't the time to get those details from her right now.

He needed to stay focused on Oasis Management

Systems. Maybe Olivia was just the person they were looking for to get the answers that they so desperately needed.

She shifted her legs beneath her. "What do you guys think is going on with this company? This seems bigger than anything I ever assumed it would be. Are people really willing to kill over ID theft?"

Axel frowned, hating the fact that he couldn't tell her the complete truth. "There are some things I'm not supposed to say. Things that you shouldn't know. Honestly, it would just put you in more danger."

Olivia nodded slowly as if she understood the sentiment.

Axel took another sip of his water, set his bottle on the table, and straightened. Then he released a long breath.

"I suppose I should get going," he said. "Do you think you're going to be okay here tonight by yourself?"

"Absolutely." She waved her hand in the air. "I'll make sure to check all my locks twice."

Just as she said the words, a rattle sounded at her door.

Maybe she'd spoken too soon.

## CHAPTER TWENTY-THREE

OLIVIA HELD her breath as she heard the noise at the door.

Was it Tristan? Had he returned? Had he tried to get in, only to discover Olivia had changed the locks?

Axel rose to his feet. "Stay here."

Olivia wasn't going to argue. She pressed herself into the couch as she waited to learn whatever that sound had come from.

Olivia didn't like the feeling of danger surrounding her. Something was going on here, and she didn't want to be part of it. But, inexplicably, she was.

The sound filled the air again.

Was that somebody knocking? Who would knock at her door at this time of night?

Axel opened the door and yanked someone into

the room, keeping one hand on the man's arm. "You recognize this guy?"

Olivia held her breath for a moment until the man with the scraggily blond beard, tattooed arms, and tanned cheeks came into focus.

She frowned when she realized this had been a misunderstanding.

"It's just Bradley," Olivia said. "He lives upstairs."

"Sorry, man." Bradley shrugged. "Didn't know you had somebody over here. I was just wondering if you had any laundry detergent I could borrow."

This was so typical of Bradley. But instead of bringing up that fact, Olivia rose to her feet and grabbed a few tabs from her cleaning closet. "Here you go."

He took them from her before raising his hands again and glancing at Axel with wide eyes. "Again, sorry to interrupt anything, man. Didn't think it was going to be this big of a deal or I would have stayed away."

"Don't worry about it, Bradley."

After he left, Olivia turned to Axel and shrugged. "Bradley is harmless. Really. Unless you're a wave and then, apparently, he can *kill it*. His words, not mine."

"Good to know." But Axel's gaze still looked dark. He remained by the door a moment, as if hesitant to leave until finally turning toward her with his lips downturned. "Okay. This is good night then. Make sure you lock the door behind me. I'm going to double check."

Olivia hid a smile. Really, it was kind of sweet to see him acting so concerned. Maybe even womanizers could have big hearts sometimes.

Still, she'd be wise to keep her distance from the man.

"Thank you again, and I'll talk to you in the morning," Olivia finally said.

He gave her a salute before stepping outside. "Good night, sweetheart."

If Olivia had another pillow in her hand, she'd throw it at him. But instead she just chuckled.

---

"SO WHAT DID YOU FIND OUT?" Rocco asked when Axel got back to the Blackout headquarters. They were meeting in the conference room again, and someone had brought pizza—with anchovies.

That had to be No-Smile Beckett. He was the only person Axel knew who liked anchovies on his pizza.

Despite that, Axel grabbed a piece. He was hungrier than he'd realized.

After taking a bite and swallowing, Axel gave his team a rundown of this evening's events.

When he finished, he grabbed a second slice and

leaned back in his seat. "How about you guys? Did anything happen after I left?"

"Not really," Rocco said. "Gabe was able to get into the computer and copy the hard drive. There was nothing there."

"Whose computer?" Axel let the salty flavor wash over his taste buds. Anchovies actually weren't half bad—but he'd never admit it to Beckett.

"Stan Bennett's. We weren't able to get into any other bedrooms."

"Stan Bennett is staying at the house next door," Axel said. "I heard him tell Olivia that."

Rocco narrowed his gaze. "It was supposed to be his room."

Axel shrugged. "I don't know when things changed —I just know what I heard."

"So our next task will be figuring out whose computer we breached," Rocco said.

Gabe flipped a pencil in his fingers. "Meanwhile, do you want me to hit another computer at tomorrow's luncheon?"

"I think it's worth a shot," Rocco said. "We all tried to eavesdrop into conversations, but no one seemed suspicious. We're going to need to think of a way to up our game."

Axel shifted, unsure how his team would react to the update he was about to give. "Olivia and I are having dinner with Stan tomorrow night."

Rocco twisted his head, his eyes narrowed with surprise. "That's interesting."

"The man really seems to like her." If Axel were being honest, he'd admit that it bothered him to see just how fond the man was of Olivia. He didn't trust anyone in the Bennett family—and for good reason.

"Maybe that connection is our best bet then," Rocco said. "If Olivia is up for it."

Axel put a piece of crust back onto his plate and wiped his mouth. He couldn't argue with that. Olivia seemed to be their connection here. "She was the one who agreed to dinner."

Gabe continued twirling the pencil between his fingers. "Are you sure you can trust Olivia?"

Axel thought about the question a moment. He remembered the sincerity in Olivia's eyes. He thought about the honest fear in her as danger had hovered too close for comfort. Could someone fake that?

He didn't think so.

"I do think we can trust Olivia," Axel finally said. "Right now, at least. But I'll remain cautious, of course."

"Good idea." Rocco nodded slowly, thoughtfully. "We need to figure out exactly what kind of questions you should ask Stan tomorrow in order to get some of those answers we need. Otherwise, the rest of us have another soirée that we'll be attending at this retreat during lunch tomorrow. Again, we'll be acting as servers. Only the best for Oasis and their staff."

Rocco offered a half eye roll. As operatives who'd put their lives on the line for the country, nothing was worse than being around pious rich folks who wanted to be waited on. But right now, it was part of their job.

Axel, for one, was glad he didn't have to serve these people. "Makes me think that I got the better end of the bargain."

Beckett stared at him, his normal glaring turning into a teasing gleam. "I have to admit, I wasn't sure if you and Olivia were going to be able to pull this whole charade off."

Axel shrugged. "What can I say? I'm that good."

The other guys chuckled at his false modesty. In all honesty, he hadn't been all that certain either. But even though Olivia had stumbled a few times, she'd managed to follow his lead as he rectified the situation.

"We'll let you think that you're just that talented." Rocco shook his head, a grin tugging at his lips.

But Beckett clearly wasn't done. "For real. You two seemed surprisingly comfortable with each other."

"You don't know what you're talking about." Axel gave him a look.

"I saw the way the two of you glanced at each other," Beckett continued, a mischievous gleam in his eyes. "You have . . . what's that word? Chemistry. Mushy, gushy chemistry."

The guys chuckled around him at the way Beckett said the words with something close to disgust.

Axel quickly shook his head. "I wouldn't say that. But it *is* kind of fun pushing her buttons."

"I know what that means." Rocco gave him a look.

Axel definitely needed to set the record straight before his team started to plan a wedding that was never going to happen. "It means nothing except that I like pushing Olivia's buttons. I mean, you've got to have some type of joy in this life, and that's mine at this very moment."

The guys ribbed him a few more minutes before Rocco stood and glanced at his watch.

"Alright, let's turn in for the night," he said. "But we'll meet again in the morning. Axel, don't forget that from here on out, you and Olivia are engaged. We don't want wind of this fake engagement getting around town. So while the Oasis Retreat is taking place on the island, you two are together—not just in front of Oasis. In front of anyone."

Axel nodded.

It sounded like he had his work cut out for him. But if he allowed himself, spending more time with Olivia might just turn out to feel more like personal time rather than work time.

# CHAPTER TWENTY-FOUR

OLIVIA COULDN'T STOP THINKING about everything that had transpired over the past two days as she worked the morning shift at The Crazy Chefette. The place was jam-packed today.

Normally, she didn't get tired on her feet. But she hadn't slept very well last night. She'd had too much on her mind.

Olivia had been too busy replaying the outing with Axel. The man . . . he was different than she'd expected. More protective. More gentle. Less of a player.

But that still didn't mean she trusted him.

She just needed to forget that look in his brown eyes when their gazes had connected.

Something about it had taken her breath away.

Then she'd listened for the sounds of someone trying to break into her place.

Someone like Tristan.

She didn't want to be paranoid, but, until she knew the scope of what was going on, she couldn't help it.

"You look chipper today."

Olivia glanced behind her as she made a fresh pot of coffee and saw Lisa standing there.

"Chipper?" She shoved the filter in place and chuckled. "I don't know about that. I feel tired."

"You have a new light in your eyes."

She did? She resisted the urge to look in the mirror. Had Axel somehow ignited a spark Olivia hadn't known she'd been lacking?

Olivia realized that Lisa had no idea what had transpired since the confrontation with Tristan behind the restaurant. She briefly considered filling Lisa in, to at least tell her about the fake engagement to Axel. It would be weird if Lisa heard from somebody else.

Olivia pressed the button to start the coffee brewing and then turned to her boss. Though she had customers to wait on, certainly she could take three minutes to give her boss an update.

"There's something that I need to tell you." Olivia's voice trembled, making her sound nervous.

She supposed she was nervous. But she hadn't expected to be *this* nervous.

Lisa continued to roll some silverware into napkins behind the counter. "What's that?"

Before she could answer, someone stepped behind her and slipped an arm around her waist.

Olivia sucked in a breath.

When she smelled the soapy scent, she knew exactly who it was.

Axel.

He kissed her temple and said, "Good morning, sweetheart."

Olivia's cheeks heated.

What was he doing? He wanted to get a rise out of her, didn't he?

Lisa's eyes widened as she looked back and forth between them. Suddenly, her silverware was forgotten. "Wait . . . you two? You're together? When did that happen?"

Olivia scowled at Axel. He'd known *exactly* what he was doing.

Well, two could play at that game.

Olivia cleared her throat, trying her best to tap into her acting skills. She had taken a couple of classes in college as a part of her liberal arts degree. But she never thought she'd use those skills for something like this.

"Axel and I actually started talking yesterday after work, and, next thing you know, here we are." She turned into his arms, rose on her tiptoes and gave him a lingering kiss on the cheek.

Axel went rigid as if frozen beneath her touch.

*Gotcha.*

She hid her grin and faced Lisa again. "Turns out, you were right. He is an all-around good guy." She waved a hand in the air.

Lisa's eyes widened as her gaze followed Olivia's left hand.

*Oh no!*

Olivia realized what she'd done and tried to hide her hand by stuffing it into the pocket of her jeans.

But it was too late. Lisa had caught sight of her engagement ring.

"And you're getting married?" Lisa grabbed Olivia's hand and studied the ring.

Olivia's cheeks heated even more. "It's a long story—"

"Not that long. When you know, you know. Right, honey?" Axel quickly recovered, pulled her closer, and winked at her as if he'd won this acting session.

She could seriously kill him right now. But she couldn't let her aggravation show through. Especially if she was going to beat him at his own game.

"There are going to be a lot of disappointed ladies here." Lisa grinned from ear to ear. "In fact, I just might lose some business from the women who come into the restaurant just to see if you were here, Axel.

But I'm so happy for you both! I never even saw this coming."

While Axel easily kept up the charade, guilt flooded Olivia. She needed to tell Lisa the truth. Certainly it wouldn't hurt to let her boss know what was really going on.

But Axel seemed to read her mind and, as he glanced at her, he shook his head as if letting her know she should stay quiet on the subject.

"Do you mind if I steal her away for a minute?" Axel took Olivia's arm. "I promise, I won't keep her long."

Lisa practically beamed as she turned to them. "Take all the time you need. The two of you being together... that just makes my day."

---

AXEL HAD to admit that he liked seeing Olivia blush. At least it was one pleasant thing in an otherwise unpleasant situation. And when she'd turned into his arms and kissed his cheek, he'd been so surprised, he'd actually lost his breath.

Although he knew Olivia was driving home a point, he wasn't left unaffected. This woman intrigued him more and more.

But for now, things had to get down to business.

He pulled Olivia to the back of the restaurant for

some privacy and glanced around to make sure it was safe. He didn't see anyone suspicious.

"Is everything okay?" Olivia looked up at him, her eyes full of questions.

He wished he could tell her everything, that he didn't have to keep the truth from her, but he needed the okay from Colton first.

He thought he could trust her, that she wasn't the type who'd spill this to anyone at Oasis. But it wasn't his call.

For now, she just needed to think all this was about identity theft.

"Listen, did you talk to anyone last night after I left your place?" Axel asked.

She shook her head. "No, I went to bed. Why?"

"You didn't tell anyone who I really was?"

"Why would I do that? What's going on?"

"You didn't answer the question..."

She bristled. "I didn't tell anyone, Axel. I'd be putting myself in just as much danger as you all are in. Now, you're scaring me. What's going on?"

He glanced around again and stepped closer. "Gabe put a tracker on one of the computers. That means we can watch everything that happens on that laptop. This morning, someone typed in 'Blackout.'"

Olivia's eyes widened. "You think you've been made? I promise, I didn't say a word. I want to bring these guys down."

As her voice began to rise, Axel shushed her and stepped closer. "I believe you. But somehow, they might be onto us."

"But if they're onto you . . . you could all be in danger."

"None of our pictures are on the site," he assured her. "They shouldn't be able to identify us. But it's all suspicious. That's for sure."

"Oh, Axel . . . I'm sorry. I don't know what to say."

He relaxed a little and rubbed her arm. "It's okay."

Axel looked up as someone stepped into the restaurant.

He sucked in a breath. What was he doing here?

## CHAPTER TWENTY-FIVE

MITCH ABRAMS, the vice president of Oasis, surveyed everyone at the restaurant before the hostess seated him at a corner table.

Even when he had a menu in his hand, he scanned the room again.

His gaze stopped on Axel and Olivia.

Axel leaned in toward Olivia, pressed a hand to her waist and murmured, "He's watching us."

He might have felt a small thrill as he felt the tremble rake through Olivia when he touched her. If he were honest with himself, he also felt a jolt whenever they touched. But he'd never admit that out loud.

Olivia seemed to scoot even closer. She lowered her voice as she asked, "Is that supposed to mean something?"

"That just means you can't look like you hate me right now."

"I don't hate you. I never said I hated you." Her voice lilted with outrage.

"Then don't act like it either." He left his hand on her waist as he continued to talk in low tones close to her.

"I think I've proven already that I can act." She lifted her brows. "I helped fool Lisa, didn't I?"

"The kiss on the cheek was a nice touch," he admitted.

There was something about being this close to Olivia that Axel liked. He could smell the honeysuckle scent she wore. Was it shampoo? He wasn't sure, but either way he liked it.

He also liked how silky Olivia's hair felt as it brushed his fingertips and how soft her skin felt.

Axel stopped his thoughts.

It had been a long time since he'd craved more of someone. He wasn't sure if he liked the feeling—or if he *should* like it, to be more accurate. If he were wise, he'd remain on guard.

For that matter, he'd been on guard for the past four years. Never letting anybody get too close.

But something about Olivia was different. Maybe it was the fact that she didn't like him. That she didn't pursue him or throw herself at him.

Or maybe it was just her sweet smile and spunky attitude.

Axel would have to think about that another time.

He glanced at Mitch again.

As he did, the man looked away and studied his menu.

Axel would stay until this guy left, just to make sure everything was okay.

Because he didn't want to take any chances . . . especially not when Olivia's life was on the line.

---

OLIVIA GLANCED AT HER WATCH. She had a couple more hours until she would head back to her apartment and get ready for the dinner date with Stan tonight.

She surveyed the restaurant and saw that all her customers were happy. So she wandered behind the breakfast counter and lifted one foot into the air. Usually, it didn't bother her to be on her feet all day. But for some reason she felt sore right now. It was probably partly anxiety about tonight's meeting.

As she'd told Axel, Stan had always liked her. But he was also a man of very strong opinions. People were either on his good side or his bad side—there were no in-betweens.

She knew that he probably wouldn't respond well if he thought that Olivia was trying to pull one over on him. And if he found out that Axel was secretly investigating his business? Then she would really be on his bad side.

Even though the man had always treated her well, there was something edgy about him still.

As one of Olivia's customers flagged her down, the restaurant suddenly went dark.

She froze and sought Lisa's gaze.

Her boss narrowed her eyes and stepped outside, probably to see if anyone else nearby had lost power. Lisa came back in a moment later and shook her head. "I don't know what happened, but it looks like we're not the only place without power."

An eerie feeling crept up Olivia's spine.

Not that there was anything nefarious about what had happened. Still, she felt uneasy.

"I'm sorry, everyone," Lisa continued. "Unless the power comes back on, we won't be able to do any drink refills or take additional orders."

Olivia wandered up toward her. "What about all the food in the back?"

"The freezer and fridge are hooked up to a generator," Lisa said. "So the food should be good for a while."

"That's good news at least."

Lisa sighed and glanced around. "We can't take any new customers."

"I'm sorry. I know you count on every day of business in the summer."

Lisa frowned. "I do. But this is out of my control."

She was right. There was nothing else she could do.

An hour later, the power still wasn't on. The energy cooperative was still trying to figure out what had happened to knock out power in a two-block radius. One of the customers dining inside the restaurant worked for the city manager and heard something about a saltwater buildup on one of the lines.

Finally, the last customer cleared out.

When they were gone, Lisa turned to Olivia. "I'm going to go pick up Julia from Skye's house. It's too hot in here for me."

"Sounds good. Why don't you let me finish up here? I have a few more dishes to load into the dishwasher. I know we can't turn it on until later, but at least that will be done."

"You don't have to do that . . ."

Olivia glanced at her watch again. "I don't mind. Really."

It definitely beat going back to her place and thinking about her dinner with Stan.

Lisa eyed her another moment before nodding. "If you're sure."

"I'm sure. Go. Get Julia. Go to the beach. Enjoy yourself. I've got this."

Lisa took her apron off and nodded. "Okay. I'll do that. I'm going to lock you in here, though."

"I'll be fine."

She watched Lisa grab her purse and leave. Then she let out a long breath.

The moment alone actually felt nice.

She quickly loaded the dishwasher, dried her hands, and then glanced around.

She'd done everything she could for now, and it was getting too hot in here.

Olivia wandered into the back to grab her purse. She had plenty of time to go home and get ready.

As she dug out her keys, she heard something behind her and froze.

Was that a footstep? Was someone else here with her?

But everyone had cleared out.

She'd checked the place herself.

Unless someone had been hiding in the closet or the restroom.

Panic rushed through her.

Before she realized what was happening, a hand covered her mouth. The man wrapped his arm around her midsection, holding her arms in place. As he did, her purse dropped to the ground.

"You're not fooling me," a gruff voice whispered in her ear.

The next instant, the man shoved her forward.

Olivia's eyes widened when she realized what he was doing.

He opened the freezer door and pushed her inside.

She sprawled on the icy-cold floor, her lungs instantly tightening.

Then she heard the door slam behind her and something being shuffled on the other side.

Without even pushing on the door, she knew she was trapped.

# CHAPTER TWENTY-SIX

AXEL PULLED up to Olivia's apartment and glanced around.

Strange. Where was her car? Maybe she had parked it on the other side of the building.

Either way, he put his keys in his pocket and hurried up the stairs to her place. He knocked on the door and waited.

There was no answer.

Was she in the shower? Maybe she hadn't heard him at the door.

He glanced at his watch and saw that he was only five minutes early. Still, maybe five minutes could be a lot when it came to women getting ready to go to dinner.

Axel took a step back and began pacing. He'd wait a few more minutes before he tried again.

But a bad feeling went up his spine.

This was probably nothing. Just him looking at worst-case scenarios. It was what he did in his line of work.

Last time he'd seen Olivia, she'd been at The Crazy Chefette working. He would guess that she most likely came right here to get ready.

After a few minutes, he knocked at the door again.

But, again, there was no answer.

Axel leaned closer to the door and listened.

The inside of the apartment sounded silent.

The bad feeling in his gut continued to grow.

He knocked one more time and then cupped his mouth with his hand and leaned toward the door. "Olivia? Are you in there?"

Still no answer.

He didn't like this.

He pulled out his phone and dialed Olivia's cell, glad she'd given him her number yesterday.

He tapped his foot as he waited.

No answer.

Of course.

Axel glanced around but didn't see anybody else nearby.

Carefully, he pulled a couple of things from his pocket and began to pick the lock. It was a skill that often came in handy.

Finally, he heard a click, and he was able to twist the handle.

He glanced around one more time. Seeing no one, Axel slipped inside the apartment and scanned the open room.

He called Olivia's name again.

But there was no response.

Quickly, he searched the place, but it didn't appear she had been here anytime recently.

Strange. Did Olivia think Axel had told her they would meet at the restaurant?

It was the only thing that he could think of.

Axel would head there and see if that's where she was.

He hoped the bad feeling in his gut was wrong.

But it usually wasn't.

---

OLIVIA TRIED the freezer door again, but it was no use.

It wouldn't budge.

Whatever that man had pushed in front of it was heavy. She pictured the cabinet where Lisa kept her spices. It wasn't that far from the freezer door. That's probably what he had used to barricade her into this space.

She let out a breath, which instantly frosted in the cold air.

Cold was an understatement. It was uncomfortably cold and getting worse by the moment.

She wished she had her phone. But it must have fallen out of her pocket when the man grabbed her. Thankfully, a small safety light buzzed overhead, allowing her to see her surroundings.

She turned and felt around, trying to figure out if there was another way out.

But there was nothing.

There were no windows. No other doors. Just one way in and out.

So what was she going to do?

Olivia had no idea.

Her thoughts continued to race.

*You're not fooling me.*

Did she recognize that voice?

She wasn't sure.

The man had obviously been trying to conceal who he was. Did that mean Olivia would have recognized it otherwise?

What did his words mean? Was someone onto her? Did they realize that she wasn't really engaged to Axel? If so, what would that mean for the future of this investigation?

The questions pounded at her temples.

She would need to think about that later. Right now, she needed to figure out how to survive.

How long would it be until somebody else came back here?

She'd told Lisa to take Julia to the beach. If Lisa actually did that, it could be another couple of hours until she returned.

Braden, Lisa's husband, also lived in the apartment over the restaurant. But Olivia had heard them saying earlier that he was working an eight-hour shift today. If Olivia's calculations were correct, it would still be several hours before he returned also.

Her heart pounded harder.

Maybe somebody else would stop by. But who?

She checked her watch.

Axel should be at her apartment trying to pick her up now.

What would he think? That she was flighty and had changed her mind?

She had no idea. Would he even think to come here looking for her?

She shivered again. Her nose was feeling numb and her fingers also.

She tucked her hands beneath her arms, trying to keep them warm and then began walking back and forth in the cramped space.

She just needed to think.

How long would she survive in here until somebody came?

She'd just watched a news story on a man who'd been locked in a freezer. What had they said?

*Sudden drops in body temperature prevent critical organs from working properly, including the brain and heart.*

Olivia had to think of a way to keep warm . . . or this place might become her grave.

## CHAPTER TWENTY-SEVEN

BEFORE AXEL HEADED to the restaurant, he tried Olivia's phone one more time.

But, again, she didn't answer.

Why wouldn't she pick up? She didn't seem like the type to let her charge run out.

As he walked toward his motorcycle, he decided to try Lisa's number.

She answered on the first ring. "Axel. What's going on?"

"Hey, I'm looking for Olivia. Have you seen her?"

"She was closing up at the restaurant last time I saw her."

"Closing up?"

"The power went out. It was just in a two-block radius. But they're working on getting it back up. What's happening?"

"I was supposed to pick her up for dinner, but she's not at her apartment."

"Oh." Lisa's voice changed from friendly to dead serious. "Maybe I should have stayed at The Crazy Chefette with her. But she was leaving right behind me and..."

"You don't know where she is now?"

"No, I'm sorry. I don't. I picked up Julia, and we went to the beach."

"If you hear from her, let me know."

"I will."

He jammed his phone back into his pocket. He would swing by The Crazy Chefette to see if Olivia had stayed there for some reason.

Axel didn't know Olivia well. But this just didn't seem like her.

And that concerned him.

He hopped on his motorcycle and headed down the road. A few minutes later, he pulled up to the restaurant.

Olivia's car wasn't in the lot.

Curious.

Despite that, Axel went to the front door and tugged on it. The place was locked, just as he'd expected it to be.

Next, he strolled to the back of the restaurant and tugged on that door also.

It was also locked.

Shading his eyes, Axel leaned into the glass, trying to see inside.

But the place looked empty.

He frowned.

It didn't appear that Olivia was here.

But if not here then where could she be?

---

THE FREEZER WAS noisy as the fan blew cold air inside.

Olivia tried to listen for anybody who might be around. But with the restaurant being closed, she doubted that would be the case. Even if she yelled, trying to catch the ear of somebody outside, she knew it was unlikely they would hear her through the thick, insulated walls. Plus, the generator was loud.

She glanced around one more time.

There were wire shelves inside the freezer. If she could take one of those apart and use one of the rods . . . maybe it would leverage the door open enough to get out. Or she could use one to try and jam the fan. Maybe it wouldn't be as cold in here if she did that.

It was worth a shot. And it was better than sitting here and just waiting.

As soon as her hands touched the metal, her skin

stuck to it. Even though her fingers were going numb, they weren't numb enough not to feel the pain with the cold.

She pulled them away quickly and rubbed them on her jeans.

She could do this.

She had no other choice.

She moved boxes of ground beef from that shelf to the shelf above it.

Then she tugged on the metal frame again.

It didn't budge.

She studied the back of the freezer and frowned.

The shelves didn't appear to come apart. Even if it was a possibility, quite a bit of frost was built up where the metal frame met the wall. The ice would be almost impossible to break through.

Olivia looked around, trying to find something she might be able to use to chip away at the thick frost.

But Lisa was immaculate with her kitchen, and this freezer area was no different.

Olivia frowned. That plan might not work.

But she couldn't give up.

She'd already thrown her body weight into the door uncountable times.

It hadn't budged.

So what was she going to do?

Nothing. There was nothing else she could do.

A cry rose in her throat.

She couldn't let despair win.

Her only hope now was that someone would find her in time.

## CHAPTER TWENTY-EIGHT

AXEL STARTED across the gravel parking lot to his motorcycle when he paused.

Something in his gut told him not to leave yet.

But he'd looked inside the restaurant and hadn't seen anyone. Of course, he couldn't see everything.

But nothing he'd seen indicated any type of struggle. And Olivia's car wasn't here either...

Despite that, Axel peered inside again. Maybe he'd missed something.

He scanned the back portion of the restaurant, trying to see everything he could.

As he glanced into the kitchen area, his breath caught.

Why did it look like a cabinet had been shoved in front of the freezer door?

The furniture was out of place in that position.

And the freezer wouldn't be able to be accessed.

At once, Axel realized what he'd missed.

What if Olivia was in that freezer?

He had to make a split-second decision.

And it was a no-brainer.

He took his jacket off and wrapped it around his arm. Quickly, he hit the glass and it shattered.

He then reached inside, unlocked the door, and rushed toward the freezer.

Wasting no time, he shoved the cabinet out of the way. "Olivia? Can you hear me?"

No response came from inside.

Axel grabbed the handle and threw the door open.

His gut clenched at what he saw inside.

Olivia was curled in a ball on the floor in the middle of the freezer.

Unmoving.

---

"OLIVIA?"

She pulled her eyes open.

As she turned, Axel came into view.

Axel? Or was she seeing things?

She didn't care. Either way, she sprang to her feet.

The next moment, Axel had her wrapped in his arms and carried her from the freezer.

She nestled herself against his warm arms, against his chest and body heat. She had been so cold. So, so cold.

"What happened to you?" he muttered.

The way he said it made it clear he wasn't expecting an answer right now.

And that was good because her teeth were chattering too much to speak.

He found a chair and put her down. Then he took his black leather jacket and placed it around her shoulders. He pulled her toward him again, clearly trying to get her warmed up.

Her teeth wouldn't stop chattering and her muscles wouldn't stop shivering.

Olivia had sat on the floor to conserve her energy. She'd stacked some boxes around her, trying to trap her body heat. She wasn't sure if it had worked.

At some point, she must have started to lose consciousness.

If Axel hadn't gotten here when he did ...

She leaned into him, never so happy to see anyone before. She wished she could speak, but it was going to be a few more minutes.

Still keeping an arm around her, Axel reached down on the floor and picked up a piece of folded paper. As he opened it, Olivia knew exactly what he would see on it.

She waited for his reaction.

"I'm sorry it's come to this," he read aloud. "Just know that I love you. I'm only doing what's best." Axel glanced at her. "What's this?"

She shivered.

"Never mind. We can talk about that later." He knelt in front of her. "How long were you in there?"

"An . . . hour . . . maybe." But Olivia's words bumped and jostled all over the place. Her mouth just wouldn't work the way she wanted.

"We should get you to the clinic."

She shook her head. "I'm fine."

"You don't look or sound fine." He pulled back just enough to look her in the eye.

"Just . . . need . . . a minute."

She just needed some warmth and then she would be okay.

"How about if I get you some hot water?"

"The . . . power . . . is . . . out. Generator on."

"Maybe the microwave is hooked up. I'll check."

Axel hurried across the kitchen.

She instantly missed his warmth. She craved more of it.

From a purely practical standpoint, of course.

Axel returned a moment later and handed her some warm water.

Apparently, the microwave did work.

He helped her hold the mug as she brought it to her lips and took a small sip.

It was like bliss.

He continued to help her until she'd drunk almost a whole cup.

Finally, her shivers died down some.

"What happened?" Axel knelt in front of her and stared her in the eye.

She recounted the story—including the man's ominous words—*You're not fooling me*. With each new detail, Axel's face got tighter and tighter.

"I don't like this," he muttered. "At all."

"Me neither."

He reached onto the floor and handed something to her. Her purse. "I found this in the kitchen."

She took it from him and placed it beside her.

But there was only one thing she could think about.

Only one thing she wanted right now.

"We've got to go meet Stan." Determination hardened her words.

Axel shook his head, his expression brooking no argument. "That's a terrible idea. We need to call him. Cancel."

"No, we can't do that. Just get me back to my place. I can change. We can still make it in time."

He stared at her another moment, uncertainty in his gaze.

And then he stood. "Are you sure? We should be filing a police report right now."

"We can do that later. Or on the way. I don't want to miss this opportunity."

He gave her a long look before taking her hand. "Then let's go."

## CHAPTER TWENTY-NINE

AXEL PUT his phone back in his pocket and continued to pace the living room of Olivia's apartment. She was taking a quick shower before getting dressed.

He glanced at the time.

They had ten minutes to get there before they were late. Olivia assured him that she was going to make it.

Axel had already called the other Blackout guys, and they were going to handle the situation that had happened at The Crazy Chefette, including calling Cassidy. But the whole thing bothered him.

What had somebody hoped to accomplish by locking Olivia in that freezer?

And who would have gone so far to do something like that?

He remembered the words from the note. *I'm sorry*

*it's come to this. Just know that I love you. I'm only doing what's best.*

Before Olivia slipped into the shower, she'd pulled out other notes also. She'd received multiple ones, each on the same kind of paper and each message vaguely threatening.

Who had sent them? Why?

Axel would have his guys look at them, to check for fingerprints.

But he didn't like any of this.

Finally, Olivia stepped from her room.

Seeing her took Axel's breath away.

She'd swept her hair back into an elegant twist. She wore a sundress with sandals and had applied light makeup over her cheeks and eyes. Not that she really needed any makeup.

He let out a low whistle. She looked great.

He wasn't sure, but Olivia might have blushed. "Thank you."

He reached out his hand, almost as if it was the most natural thing in the world to do. "Are you ready?"

She nodded and hesitated a moment before slipping her hand into his. "Let's go."

He held tight to her as they stepped outside.

Axel told himself he was doing so as part of an act, so people would think that they were engaged. But another part of him liked knowing Olivia was close. He liked knowing she was there and that she was okay.

Axel paused outside and stared at his motorcycle. "I don't know where your car is. I told the guys that, and they're going to look for it."

"We can ride your motorcycle again."

He tilted his head at her. "Are you sure?"

She'd seemed hesitant when he'd given her a ride back to her apartment. This ride would be even longer.

"I'm positive. As long as I can wear that helmet again—and maybe a jacket."

"Of course."

He opened the back compartment of his motorcycle and handed her an extra helmet. Olivia slipped it on, and Axel double-checked to make sure the latch beneath her chin was properly fastened. Then he helped her into his jacket.

After they climbed on his bike, he twisted his head toward her. "You're going to need to hold on to me."

"Of course." Olivia placed her hands at his waist.

"Tighter." Axel started the engine.

Again, Olivia hesitated a moment before wrapping her arms around his waist.

When he was confident that she was holding on tight, he rolled the throttle and accelerated onto the street.

They were going to get to Stan's place right on time.

Thankfully, it wasn't that long of a drive.

Because he found himself liking the feel of Olivia's arms around him a little too much.

AS OLIVIA LEANED INTO AXEL, she felt his tight muscles beneath her fingertips.

She tried not to revel in the feeling. But it was hard not to.

Just like it was hard not to breathe in the scent of his leather jacket.

She knew exactly why women tripped all over Axel Hendrix.

He was one of *those* guys.

He had all the right things in place to make women go crazy. The looks. The smile. The personality. Even the style.

And he'd saved her today. That was something she would always be grateful for, no matter how infuriating the man could be.

But a sick feeling churned in her stomach as she remembered their upcoming dinner. As she remembered the person who'd locked her in that freezer. As she remembered the notes that had been left.

This entire situation was dangerous. Olivia knew that going into this. But that didn't help calm her down now.

Instead, she closed her eyes and let the wind whip around her. She let herself lean into Axel and trust his driving skills.

With anyone else, she would be nervous that they would be in an accident.

But something about Axel was different.

Way too soon, they pulled up to the beach house where Stan was staying. He'd gotten his own place. As CEO of the company, that was no surprise.

Axel climbed off the motorcycle before helping her off.

As he did, their gazes caught.

This man had saved her life. And had come to her rescue more than once. Maybe she could give the guy some slack. Besides, Olivia could stand there staring at him all day and be perfectly content.

But the sound of his phone ringing cut through the moment.

He excused himself and put it to his ear. As soon as she saw his expression, she knew it was bad news.

He slid his phone back into his pocket as he turned to her.

"That was Colton. They've been checking into Stan's background a little more. It turns out he has ties with the Russian mafia."

Olivia sucked in a breath.

The Russian mafia?

That was something she hadn't expected.

## CHAPTER THIRTY

AXEL'S JAW tightened as he realized just how deeply this all might run. With every new fact that emerged, it became clear this was a dangerous situation.

Too dangerous for Olivia.

He turned toward her and frowned. "We need to call Stan and cancel."

"But we're already here," Olivia said.

Still, based on what Axel had just learned, this wasn't the kind of guy Olivia needed to be around—even if she had saved his life and the man did think the world of her. He was still dangerous.

"This is our best chance to get information," Olivia said. "We don't want to waste it."

Axel studied her face. The moonlight hit her cheeks, illuminating the lovely lines of her profile. He could smell hints of her flowery perfume as it mixed with the salty ocean breeze.

She really was a sight to behold.

Not only that, but she was determined.

Olivia really wanted to put these people behind bars, didn't she? Was there more to that story than she was letting on?

It didn't matter. Axel still thought this was a terrible idea.

"We'll think of another way." He reached for her arm and tugged her back toward his bike.

As he did, he sensed movement in the distance.

When he looked up, he spotted Stan on the front deck waiting for them.

Axel bit back a groan. Great.

Now that Stan had seen them, leaving would be awkward—and possibly suspicious.

Olivia stepped closer, her gaze locked on his. "We can do this. *I* can do this."

She was determined to carry through with this, and Axel knew he wouldn't be able to talk her out of it.

He released his breath before nodding. "Okay. But we play this by my rules. You don't go anywhere alone with him. You follow my lead. And at the first sign of danger, we leave."

A small smile tugged at the corner of her lips. "Understood."

Axel reached his hand out, and Olivia fit hers into

his. He was getting used to this. Getting used to the feel of her skin against his.

But he shouldn't. If he were smart, he would set aside any emotions or feelings. He wasn't in the market for a girlfriend, but pretending was starting to hit too close to home. That kiss on the cheek Olivia had given him had just about brought him to his knees.

But he couldn't think about his reaction now. Too much was at stake.

As they reached the steps, Stan smiled down at them. "It's great to see you two. I was afraid you weren't going to make it, but, just like always, you're right on time."

Olivia let out a chuckle beside him. "If there's one thing I'm good at, it's being on time."

She and Axel exchanged another glance before following Stan into his house.

But every time Axel thought about this man having affiliations with the Russian mafia, he just kept thinking what a bad idea this was.

---

DINNER so far had gone off without a hitch, as the saying went. Stan had brought his personal chef with him, who had prepared salmon, risotto, and asparagus. The food exceeded expectations, but their conversation was rather mundane.

Olivia wanted this to be more than a time to catch up with Stan, however.

She wanted answers.

She wiped her mouth before placing her napkin back into her lap. "So, anything new at the company?"

Stan took a sip of his whiskey. The drink was the man's favorite, and it seemed he always had some on hand to offer anyone who came into his office.

"Things are better than ever," Stan said.

"What exactly is it that you do?" Axel took a sip of his water before leaning back in his chair.

Stan took another sip of his drink. "We manage the computer systems for hotels—reservations, check-ins, checkouts. We can monitor security cameras, keycards—we can see everyone who comes and goes from a room and how often. It's even been used to help the police solve a few cases."

"That sounds pretty amazing." Axel nodded as if impressed.

"It is. We have three hundred employees who work to continue developing and maintaining software as well as offer support to the hotels utilizing our program."

"What's the future have in store for the company?" Olivia asked.

Stan raised his eyebrows. "Funny you ask. We're actually expanding."

"To do what?" Olivia pressed.

"We'll have a computer-based concierge service that will help customers know what they can do in the area."

As Stan continued to talk, Olivia nibbled on her bottom lip.

A concierge service? It seemed like Oasis would be able to track every move people staying at the hotels made before too long.

And that was a scary thought.

## CHAPTER THIRTY-ONE

AS SOON AS they finished eating, someone knocked at Stan's door.

"Excuse me a minute," Stan said. "Why don't you two enjoy the view from the deck while I see who's here."

"Of course," Olivia said, rising from the table.

Before she and Axel stepped outside, Olivia glanced back.

Stan opened the door, and a man with dark hair stood on the other side.

Who was that man?

Olivia had never seen him before.

Based on their body language, the conversation was tense.

Axel tugged her out onto the deck, his gaze following hers. "Know who he is?"

"I have no idea," she whispered. "You?"

"No, but you have to wonder what they're talking about."

Just as Axel said those words, Stan looked back at them and his eyes narrowed. The next instant, he stepped outside with his guest.

Olivia headed farther out on the deck, wondering if they could hear anything from that vantage point.

But the wind was too strong.

Still, it was nice to get away from some of the tension she'd felt around the table.

Olivia was fairly certain she was the only one who felt it. Stan certainly didn't seem to notice anything. She hoped she was putting up a good act and that he wasn't suspicious about her relationship with Axel.

But every time she closed her eyes, she remembered the threat that man had made before shoving her into the freezer. Someone knew her secret. Had said she wasn't fooling him.

If the wrong person found out, she knew it would mean trouble.

She thought she could pull this off, but now she was starting to doubt herself.

Axel stood behind her and put his hands on her shoulders as they stared out at the ocean. He began using his fingers to work out the kinks in her neck muscles.

"You're starting to look tense," he whispered.

His fingers were practically magical as he worked out all the tightness in her back.

"I'm trying to stay loose," she said.

"If we want to pull this off, we can't try. We have to just do this. Remember, Stan is a dangerous man, especially if he's betrayed."

Olivia frowned. She knew Axel's words were correct. But she thought she'd been doing pretty well.

She could get used to feeling Axel's hands massaging her taut muscles. Could get used to this closeness.

In fact, she was starting just to get used to Axel in general.

That probably wasn't a good thing.

Soon, this whole charade would be over, and they would both return to their lives. Which was exactly what she wanted.

Or was it?

Axel glanced to the side. "Stan came back inside. He's watching us right now."

"What do you want me to do? Kiss you again or something?"

"Maybe. It's not a bad idea." He moved around to face her, remaining close.

Warmth flooded her cheeks. "Really?"

Axel raised his eyebrows as his hands cupped her neck and jaw. As his fingers played in her hair. As the breeze brushed their skin, making everything feel more alive.

"We don't want him getting suspicious now, do we?" Axel murmured.

Olivia's throat felt dry as she stared at Axel's lips. "I suppose we don't."

The next moment, he leaned toward her and their lips met. As they did, something exploded inside Olivia. She found herself clutching his chest—and not wanting to let go.

This was way better than a peck on the cheek.

Unfortunately, the kiss ended as quickly as it started.

It left her wanting more.

Which was trouble.

So much trouble.

---

"I WAS WORRIED for a moment that the two of you were having some problems."

Axel stepped back and turned toward the sound.

Stan had walked onto the deck, and they hadn't even heard him.

Olivia scooted into Axel's outstretched arms and stood close to him. "What do you mean?"

"Things just seemed tense between the two of you.

But looking at you now, I can see that you are perfect together."

Axel swallowed hard at the man's words. He was glad they had pulled it off—maybe a little too well. Or was that because neither of them was acting?

"Perfect together?" Axel said. "That's what I like to hear."

"There's something about the way that you look at each other," Stan shrugged. "You know, I've always thought of you like a daughter, Olivia."

"That means a lot to me." She smiled.

The man did seem to have a soft spot for her, even if he was known as a shark by most in the business world.

"I mean it. You were brilliant at your job. I hated to see you go. Just like I hate to see you as a waitress now. You're wasting your talents."

Olivia had mentioned her current job to Stan while they'd eaten dinner.

"It's not permanent," she told him. "Just something to hold me over until I figure my future out."

Stan nodded slowly, not even pretending to understand. "Speaking of your future, I could never really see you permanently with my son. Quite honestly, I always thought that you could do better. Selfishly, I wanted the two of you together though."

Was this their opportunity to ask some questions? Olivia seemed to read his mind.

"I thought the two of you had turned over a new leaf," she started. "After all, someone said Tristan was going to step in and help with the company."

Stan laughed and shook his head. "I would never trust him to do that. I thought I raised him to be a good boy, but Tristan only wants things for free. He doesn't know what it's like to work for something. He thinks good things should just fall into his lap."

Axel's heart pounded in his ears as he anticipated where this conversation might go.

"If Tristan doesn't work for you, what will he do?" Olivia asked.

Stan shrugged as if he didn't have a worry in the world. "That's a good question. I know my son wants to impress me. But he's had his whole life to do that, and he hasn't been successful yet."

Axel rubbed his throat. He wasn't really surprised by Stan's words. But Tristan was bound to resent his father's lack of faith in him.

"I'm sorry to hear that," Olivia finally said.

Stan narrowed his gaze as his eyes latched onto Olivia's. "You know how I feel when people disappoint me. I don't handle it well."

Axel swallowed hard. Was Stan onto them?

If he found out about their fake engagement, exactly how would he react?

Would the act be enough to warrant payback . . . and would that payback be violent?

## CHAPTER THIRTY-TWO

"NOW, for dessert I would like you both to join me at the company's social this evening." Stan clasped his hands together, turning from their serious conversation to something obviously more casual.

Concern ricocheted through Axel. He and Olivia needed to get out of here and away from these people. All Axel wanted was to whisk his fake fiancée away, and he'd been counting down the moments until he could do so.

Now this.

"We can't possibly impose," Axel finally said.

"You wouldn't be imposing. You would be my guest. I insist. In fact, if you don't come, I will be insulted."

Axel glanced at Olivia and saw that her face looked pale.

He wasn't sure how he could gracefully get out of

this. Plus, it would be a good opportunity to learn more information. As long as it didn't put Olivia in danger.

"That sounds great," Olivia rushed.

Of course she'd said that. Because she was determined to see this through. Axel wasn't sure whether he admired that or if he wanted to shake some sense into her.

"Whatever you want to do, sweetie." He tightened his embrace and pulled Olivia closer.

Funny how natural that felt. In fact, sometimes this didn't feel like an act at all anymore.

"Wonderful. As you know, it's just next door. How about if I meet you there in ten minutes?"

Axel thanked him again for the dinner before taking Olivia's hand and walking with her toward his motorcycle. He waited until they reached it before he turned to her.

His hands went to her waist as if that was where they were supposed to be. But he knew that there was nobody out here watching them right now. Yet he still didn't drop his hold on her.

"How are you doing?" he asked. "How are you *really* doing?"

Olivia was out of breath. "I'm a little more tense than I'd like. But I'm willing to push through that. You heard some of the things that he said. We could be getting closer to answers."

Axel frowned. Maybe they were. But at what cost?

"Okay then," he finally said. "Let's ride over there. I'd rather have my motorcycle close."

They climbed on, and Axel tried not to marvel at how well Olivia fit behind him. Instead, he backed his bike out before heading down the lane, onto the highway, and into the neighboring driveway. Each home on this stretch had its own lane.

Before they went inside the other house, Olivia tugged his hand and turned to him.

Her gaze was serious as she looked up at him. "I can't let him find out we're faking this."

Axel nodded. He'd realized the same thing. "I know. Our lives might depend on it."

"Exactly." She nodded, not even bothering to hide the fear in her eyes. "Just so that we're on the same page."

"If we're not on the same page, then we're both dead." He hated to say it like that, but he needed to drive home the reality of this situation.

With a nod to each other, they stepped into the house.

As they did, Axel's phone buzzed with a text. He looked at the screen, trying not to show any emotion or give away what he'd just learned.

But another one of those missing women had just been found.

Dead.

THIS PARTY LOOKED MUCH like the one the night before. The same people. The same vibe. The same appearance by the Blackout crew acting as servers.

Olivia stayed close to Axel, just as she'd promised. She made small talk with several people, trying to look at ease and relaxed. But she felt anything but. They needed answers, and those very answers seemed to be slow in coming.

As she and Axel stood off to the side of the room, she spotted Miranda in the distance. The woman looked toward them, but her eyes were on Axel.

"Long time no see." Her gaze flickered at Olivia. "Don't you look ... cute."

She knew that was the woman's way of subtly putting her down. Sure, Olivia wasn't wearing a designer dress, but she didn't need to in order to feel good about herself.

"And who is this with you?" She looked up at Axel and batted her eyes.

"This is my fiancé, Axel. Axel, this is Miranda."

Miranda extended her hand as if she wanted him to kiss the top. Instead, Axel gave her a quick handshake.

Miranda turned back to Olivia and a flicker of dislike flashed across her gaze. "Who would have ever thought we would run into you here?"

Olivia forced a tight smile. "It's a small world, now, isn't it?"

"It sure is." She nodded toward the beach. "But this island is a beautiful place. I hope you're happy here."

Olivia stepped closer to Axel and rested her left hand on his chest. "Oh, I am. I'm very happy."

Miranda's smile dimmed some. "Well, I'm going to keep going. But I hope to catch up with you later." As she said the words, her gaze was clearly on Axel and not Olivia.

That wasn't surprising.

"She's a real handful," Axel muttered.

"Tell me about it." Olivia fought a frown.

Miranda had been "in love" with Tristan when Tristan had decided to date Olivia. The woman had held it against Olivia ever since.

Just then, someone else wandered up to Olivia—Cleveland, Stan's assistant. He began chatting about restaurants on the island. As they talked, Miranda cornered Axel again.

Olivia tried not to eavesdrop on the conversation, but she couldn't miss the way that Miranda giggled at everything Axel said.

Her annoyance turned into a touch of jealousy.

Jealousy? That couldn't be it. Because she and Axel weren't really engaged. They were just faking this.

What if Axel felt something for somebody like Miranda? Wasn't she his type? The overly pretty kind who was outgoing and pushy? That was the type Olivia had always seen around Axel at The Crazy Chefette.

"So what do you think?"

She turned her attention back to Cleveland and realized she hadn't heard anything he'd said. "I'm sorry, run that past me one more time?"

"It's about restaurants on the island..."

Olivia tried to focus on this conversation. But as Miranda giggled behind her again, Olivia realized it was going to be harder than she expected.

## CHAPTER THIRTY-THREE

AXEL WANTED to back out of this conversation with Miranda. But the woman wouldn't let him. Every time he tried to wrap things up, she came back with something new.

He knew her type. The aggressive ones.

They were the ones Axel knew to keep his distance from.

Instead, he wanted to get back to his conversation with Olivia.

He heard her talking politely behind him.

His mind drifted back to that kiss they'd shared. Feeling her lips against his . . . it was everything he'd thought it would be and more. Her mouth had tasted sweet. Her skin had felt soft.

But it had been fake, he reminded himself. There was nothing real about it.

He shook his head. He couldn't let his mind go there. He *wouldn't*—not if he was smart.

As there was a brief break in the conversation, Axel reached for Olivia's hand. "I'm sorry to interrupt, but I think I see somebody flagging me down over there."

Olivia glanced in the direction he pointed and frowned with confusion.

They both politely excused themselves before wandering across the room.

"Is everything okay?" she asked Axel.

"I needed to get away for a minute."

She glanced back at Miranda. "I figured she was just the kind of woman who met all the items on your checklist."

"Well, for one thing, I'm engaged to you. And for the second thing, no, she's not."

An unreadable emotion fluttered through Olivia's gaze. "I guess things surprise me every day then."

He started to say something else when someone else walked up beside them.

Stan.

"Axel . . . I was just talking to my business manager—about insurance, of all things. Then I remembered that was your field. We have something that we'd love to run past you. I've been thinking about switching our umbrella policy . . ."

Axel felt his back muscles stiffen. "I couldn't possibly leave Olivia alone."

"Of course you can. She's a big girl. I'm sure she'll be fine by herself for a few minutes."

How could Axel argue with him without giving anything away?

"It's okay." Olivia squeezed his forearm, her gaze seeming to signal that she wanted him to go. "I'll just stay here and grab a drink. No big deal."

Axel stared at her another moment longer. Leaving her side was the last thing he wanted to do. But there was no way to get out of this without seeming suspicious.

After hesitating a second longer, he nodded. "Okay then. Let's go."

But as he walked away with Stan, Axel's gaze met Rocco's. He tried to let his friend know they needed to keep an eye on Olivia.

And now he was going to have to fake his knowledge about the insurance industry . . . and pray he wasn't made in the process.

---

OLIVIA TOOK another sip of her sweet tea. Her head was beginning to pound. Maybe she should have requested that she go to the clinic after being locked in the freezer.

But it was too late for that now.

Nonetheless, as soon as Axel emerged from this

meeting with Stan and Cleveland, she might need to ask him to take her home. Maybe today had been too much, after all.

Olivia wondered if there were any updates. She knew Blackout had taken over and called the local police to let them know what happened at the restaurant. She'd guess that the police were searching for fingerprints or for any security camera footage.

But she'd have to wait to find out if they had discovered anything.

She glanced down the hallway where Axel had disappeared. Funny how she missed him. They were becoming just a little too comfortable together. Which was crazy. She needed to keep her distance.

"Would you like some bruschetta?"

She looked up and saw a tray in front of her. Her gaze met the man holding them.

His name was Beckett, if she remembered correctly.

Based on the way the man stared at her now, he was silently asking if she needed any help.

"Thank you, but I'm fine."

He stared at her a moment longer before nodding. "Understood. Let me know if you change your mind."

She rubbed her arms and glanced around again.

She was going downhill fast. If she'd had more time, she might have looked up some side effects or symptoms of frostbite or hypothermia. But she hadn't had the opportunity. And now she had a growing headache and her knees were even beginning to feel wobbly.

She frowned and glanced around.

As she did, someone else—Mitch Abrams—wandered up to her for some chitchat. She tried to respond to all his questions, but her mind just wasn't there.

She excused herself and wandered out onto the deck. At least the breeze was refreshing out here as it hit her face. Everybody else had gravitated inside, which was fine by her.

She really hoped Axel hurried up. She rubbed her temples at the thought.

Just then, Olivia heard a commotion inside.

She stepped toward the patio door, trying to get a glance at what was happening. Nearly everybody at the party had huddled together to look at something on the floor.

Had someone passed out?

A bad feeling crept up her spine.

She was about to step inside when somebody cupped her elbow. "You look like you need to sit down. You're not looking good."

Whose voice was that?

It wasn't Axel's.

She tried to look over, to see who was beside her.

But her gaze was blurry.

Then everything went black around her.

## CHAPTER THIRTY-FOUR

AXEL HEARD the commotion and rushed back into the living room.

He pushed through the crowd in time to see that someone had collapsed.

Rocco knelt beside the man—Mitch—examining him. "Everybody back. Give him space."

Axel scanned the crowd for Olivia.

Where was she?

He hadn't been gone that long.

He pushed past the cluster of people until he found Beckett. "Where did she go?"

"Last time I saw her she was headed toward the deck. Do you want me to help look for her?" He kept his voice low as he asked the question.

"Not yet. But I'll signal you if I need you. No need to break your cover unless you have to."

Axel prayed that this was some type of misunderstanding.

But that was yet to be determined.

As he stepped outside, he felt his stomach sink.

Nobody was out here.

So where had Olivia gone? Had she somehow slipped to the bathroom in the middle of all this?

His instincts told him no.

Wasting no time, Axel darted back into the house. He didn't want to draw any attention to himself. Not unless he absolutely had to.

But he had to find Olivia.

He hurried down the opposite hallway, toward the area where he'd seen Tristan take her last night.

Without bothering to knock, he opened doors and searched inside.

But Olivia wasn't in any of those rooms either.

He glanced out each of the windows he came across but saw no movement outside.

If someone had grabbed her, they hadn't taken her far.

Not yet at least.

Axel was going to give himself five more minutes to look for her.

And if he didn't find Olivia by then, then he would rally the troops.

Even if it cost him this entire investigation.

Because Olivia was worth it.

OLIVIA TRIED to pull her eyes open, but her eyelids were so heavy.

Something was wrong.

This was more than frostbite or hypothermia.

She almost felt like . . . she'd been drugged.

Consciousness came and went.

But she felt like somebody was moving her. Carrying her.

Was it Axel? Had he come back to help her?

She tried to pull her eyes open long enough to focus. But it was no use.

Everything around her was blurry.

The next instant, the movement stopped. She felt something soft beneath her.

She wanted to cry for help. Nothing would leave her lips.

Silence surrounded her.

Had her rescuer—or abductor—left?

She wanted to open her eyes and check.

But she couldn't.

Instead, she succumbed to her drowsiness and everything around her went black again.

## CHAPTER THIRTY-FIVE

AXEL TORE DOWN THE STAIRS. He hadn't seen Olivia outside. That meant she still had to be in this place. Or maybe even next door.

It was possible she could have crossed the sand dunes to Stan's place in this amount of time.

Axel knew he shouldn't have brought her here. He should have refused. Said they could find another way to get answers.

But it was too late for that.

Right now, he had to find Olivia.

The second level of the house was mostly bedrooms. Just as he'd done on the third floor, he opened every door without apology.

And just as on the third floor, every room was empty.

Every second that passed and he didn't find her, his panic intensified.

He'd check one more floor and then his five minutes were up. He would let his team know what was going on.

Out of all the people surrounding Mitch on the floor, had Tristan or Leo been there?

Axel tried to picture the scene again, but he wasn't 100 percent sure. He'd been solely focused on finding Olivia.

But his team would know.

He went down the last flight of stairs to the first floor. Some bedrooms were located on this level as well as a game room. He went to the left first and checked the two bedrooms there.

Empty.

His heart beat harder.

He rushed across the hall and into the next wing.

The first room was empty.

He threw open the door to the second room.

Someone lay on a couch there, her hand draped off the side and her body appearing lifeless.

Was that Olivia?

---

"OLIVIA? OLIVIA?"

Someone shook her.

She tried to pull her eyes open, but they still felt heavy. Like it was a chore to even try to prop them open.

"Olivia, wake up. It's me. Axel."

Axel? She tried again to force her eyes open.

Through her blurred vision, she thought she saw Axel leaning over her.

Her eyes tried to close, but Axel's prodding voice wouldn't let her drift off.

"What happened to you, Olivia?"

She wished she could tell him.

But she didn't know.

Her head swirled, and confusion gripped her.

A voice sounded behind Axel.

"I know what you're thinking. But I came down into my room and found her like this."

Olivia's insides tightened.

Tristan. That was Tristan's voice.

But why would he say that? That hadn't been what had happened.

Right?

Her thoughts were so hazy. If only the fog would clear and allow a lucid thought to form.

"You're saying you came down here and found Olivia in your room?" Anger tinged Axel's voice.

"That's right. I put the blanket over her and gave her some space. I didn't want people to think I wasn't a gentleman. Figured she'd had too much to drink and needed to sleep it off."

"She didn't have any alcohol."

"I thought maybe she'd changed her ways. Is she okay?"

Olivia wanted to move her lips. She wanted to answer him.

But she couldn't.

"Go get her a bottle of water for me," Axel said.

Olivia heard nothing else, so she assumed that Tristan left.

Axel shifted and sat beside her on the couch, pulling her into his lap.

Tenderly, he kissed the top of her head. "It's going to be okay. I'm going to figure out what happened."

And somehow, she knew that he would.

Olivia was safe now.

Knowing that, she closed her eyes.

There was no need to fight her drowsiness anymore.

## CHAPTER THIRTY-SIX

AXEL HAD to use every ounce of his self-control to stay in check. What he wanted was to go off on Tristan. To demand answers.

But, right now, Olivia needed him more.

He gently stroked her hair as she rested with her head against his chest.

She'd clearly been drugged.

It was the only reason she'd be in this state right now. But she was starting to come to. He would give her a few more minutes.

Then he would need to call for a way to get her either to the clinic or home. He had a feeling she was going to refuse the clinic.

Axel thought she was okay. That it had just been some type of sedative.

But if he hadn't arrived when he had, what would have happened to her?

Would Olivia have been the next woman taken?

Was this what had happened to those other missing women?

Anger burned inside Axel at the thought.

It made sense.

The only thing he'd seen her drinking was tea. Was there some type of tasteless sedative someone had sneaked into her beverage?

That's how it appeared. But he would need to do more research.

Tristan appeared with a bottle of water and handed it to him.

Axel nudged Olivia awake again, twisted the top off, and held the bottle to her lips. "See if you can drink some of this."

She blinked several times before leaning forward and taking a small sip. As soon as she did, a coughing fit seized her.

Axel needed to give her a few more minutes before he asked her to try again.

"So you're telling me you didn't bring Olivia down here?" Axel turned to Tristan and waited for his answer.

"I'm telling you that I came down here and found her on the couch. I thought she'd come to see me. No offense."

Axel clenched his jaw, holding back a sharp retort. "Did you see anybody come down here with her? Or did you pass anyone when you came down?"

"No. I didn't." A vein popped out on Tristan's forehead.

He clearly didn't appreciate being questioned.

"I was just coming down to get my EpiPen," Tristan continued. "Mitch had an allergic reaction to shellfish, apparently."

Axel stared at Tristan another moment, not believing his story.

He'd need to clarify that fact with his team later.

But for now, he held the bottle up to Olivia's lips again.

"Come on," he murmured. "Drink it."

She took a couple more sips and managed to keep them down this time.

But Axel knew there was no way he could get her home on his motorcycle.

Nor could he risk calling any of the Blackout guys.

So he called the next best person.

He called Cassidy to see if she might be able to give them a ride back.

Maybe by the time she got here, Olivia would be lucid.

OLIVIA TOOK another sip of water as she sat on the exam table at the Lantern Beach Medical Clinic.

Cassidy had insisted on taking her here. They needed to know what she'd been drugged with. But Olivia had begged her not to press charges.

She knew if Cassidy went around asking questions the whole operation would blow up.

She could press charges later.

Once Blackout had more answers.

Cassidy hadn't liked it, but she hadn't said she was going to investigate either.

Axel dutifully sat in the chair near her bed, watching her every move as if searching for a sign that she needed help. The doctor had left and given her instructions to rest for a few more minutes before they released her. The good news was that all her vitals were fine.

Her head still pounded and her tongue felt dry, but she was much better than she'd been just an hour ago.

"Why would someone drug me?" Olivia rubbed her temples, unable to comprehend the thoughts.

Something flashed in Axel's gaze. What was that? He was hiding something from her, wasn't he?

"I don't know exactly what they were planning," he finally said.

"But you have a guess. What's going on, Axel?"

He let out a long breath before murmuring, "You should just drink your water."

"Axel . . . what aren't you telling me?"

He let out another sigh as he glanced at her. She could see the guilt in his gaze. The tug of emotions as if he had a battle going on inside him.

"Olivia . . . I'm sorry to admit this, but there's more to this than identity theft."

Her back stiffened. She set her water on the table again and turned toward Axel, unsure if she'd heard correctly. "What?"

"Six women have gone missing over the past four months from various hotels up and down the East Coast."

"What?"

He nodded. "The only thing that connects these women is Oasis Management Systems. The company manages the computer check-ins for each of those hotels."

She sucked in a breath. "So this isn't some type of white-collar crime. This is abduction."

Axel somberly nodded. "It is."

Her gaze met his. "Why didn't you tell me this?"

"It wasn't my call. We weren't sure about your intentions, and we couldn't risk you using this information as leverage. It wasn't that we didn't want to trust you. But the stakes were high."

She crossed her arms and shook her head. "I should have known about that before I got involved. You should have told me."

"Would it have changed your mind?"

She rubbed her forehead as she felt another headache coming on. "That's a good question—and beside the point. I don't know."

Axel leaned closer. "Look, I'm sorry. I really am. That's why I insisted on being with you the whole time."

She shook her head, still unable to comprehend the scope of everything going on. "I just can't believe this. Somebody at that company may be involved with human trafficking? That's terrible."

"We don't know for sure what's happening with these women. But two of them are now dead. We don't have any time to waste."

She lowered her head as the pounding there worsened.

"Look, Olivia. I'm sorry. I really am. When I saw that you were missing tonight . . ." Axel's voice caught.

Olivia looked up. "What? What happened when you found out that I was missing?"

Maybe she shouldn't put him on the spot. But she really wanted to know.

And for that reason, she decided to wait it out and see what he had to say.

## CHAPTER THIRTY-SEVEN

AXEL FELT the knot form in his throat. This wasn't something he talked about. It wasn't something that he wanted to talk about. But now that he'd opened that door, he needed to finish his thought.

"I was worried they'd taken you too," he said. "I'm sorry I put you in that position."

"That's what almost happened, wasn't it? I was drugged and somehow ended up in that room. If you hadn't shown up when you did..."

Axel felt his jaw tighten. "My guess is that someone was going to try to arrange some type of transportation for you. It was only a matter of time."

"But we have no idea who, do we?"

"We don't."

"Tristan?"

"We're still investigating his claim that he was

getting an EpiPen. I haven't been able to debrief with the rest of the guys yet. They need to wrap up their duties first."

"I see..."

He reached forward and squeezed her hand. "I'm sorry about all this."

Olivia nodded slowly, almost as if she didn't believe him.

"Who are you, Axel Hendrix?"

He looked over at her, unsure if he'd heard the question correctly. "What do you mean?"

"I mean, I'm trying to figure you out. Are you the womanizing man I thought you were when we first met? Are you the loyal friend to those closest to you? I just can't figure you out."

He thought about her question as tumultuous thoughts tossed in his head. How much should he say?

He never shared his story with anybody.

But should he?

He felt like he was standing on a precipice right now. He needed to decide if he was going to retreat into the aloof but safe person he'd become lately or if he was going to open up and allow himself to possibly get hurt.

OLIVIA TOUCHED the engagement ring on her finger as she waited for Axel's response.

He glanced down and frowned as he looked at that piece of jewelry. His gaze darkened as if bad memories had seized him.

If Olivia's hunches were correct, this ring had a history.

One that Axel would rather forget.

After a few minutes of thought, Axel finally said, "I'm not the person I used to be."

Olivia picked up her water bottle again and took a sip. She was surprised he'd even said that much.

When she asked the question, she had no idea how Axel might respond. But she truly was curious. The two of them knew each other on a very surface level. But she wanted to know more. She wanted to go deeper.

"Who did you use to be?" Her question came out quietly, almost as a whisper.

Axel pressed his lips together before saying, "I used to be the person you said I was. I enjoyed the attention of women. It fed my ego. I work a high-risk job, so I made some high-risk choices in my dating life."

"You're saying you're not like that anymore?"

"I'm saying that I was like that until I met Mandy."

Olivia sucked in a quick breath. She desperately wanted to hear his story, but she didn't want to push him.

His gaze looked hooded—almost tortured—as he stared off in the distance. "I met Mandy through a mutual friend, and we hit it off. As soon as we got together, I didn't look at any other woman. Mandy was the only one I wanted to be with. In fact, six months after we met, we got married—right before I went on a three-month deployment."

"What happened?"

"I got back from deployment, and I was home for a good six months. The two of us were happy. Sure, we had some kinks to work out. Whenever you have to learn to live with somebody, that's the case. But we were doing okay. I thought so, at least."

Olivia waited, anxious to see where Axel was going with his story but giving him space to collect his thoughts.

"I went out to sea for another six-month deployment, and all I thought about was getting home to Mandy and how I couldn't wait to see her. She had this way of lighting up a room whenever she walked in. She just somehow made life feel better. But things weren't the same when I got home this time."

"What changed?"

"She told me that she wanted a divorce. And before I could even really contest it, I was served with the papers. I tried to talk her out of it, but Mandy had met somebody else. In fact, she met him and started dating him while I was stationed overseas."

"She cheated on you?"

He nodded. "Even worse, she had gotten pregnant. She wasn't at all the person I thought she would be. I thought she could handle the time I was away, but, apparently, she couldn't. So I became another statistic."

"What do you mean?"

"I mean that more than 90 percent of marriages for Navy SEALs end in divorce, and I was determined not to be that person. But then I felt helpless to stop it. I couldn't do anything to change her mind, and since she was pregnant . . . it almost seemed futile."

"I'm sorry, Axel."

"I hit a real low in my life, to say the least. After I met Mandy, I felt like I had purpose in my life. I had a reason to come home. Something to look forward to. Then she was gone."

"What turned you around?"

"Ty Chambers."

"Police Chief Chambers' husband?"

"As you know, he used to be a SEAL. When he got out, he started something called Hope House here. I was actually in one of the first groups he brought in to Hope House."

"I thought that was for injured war vets."

"It is. But not all injuries are the physical sort."

"I see. And it sounds like being at Hope House really changed you?"

"It did. I was a total wreck. And after talking to Ty,

he made me realize that I needed to have a greater purpose in my life. It was a slow process, not something that happened overnight. But I started going to church. Slowly, I got my life back together. And I realized that I didn't ever want it to go back to the way it had been."

Olivia's heart pounded in her ears as she listened to his story. There really was more to Axel Hendrix than she'd thought. More to the motorcycle-riding woman magnet than she'd ever guessed.

"Thank you for sharing that with me."

He nodded slowly. "It sounds like I've already kept too much from you. After this, you should probably stay away from Oasis. The stakes are too high."

"That's not your choice."

His gaze locked with hers. "I don't want anything to happen to you."

"It won't. Because you'll be there."

## CHAPTER THIRTY-EIGHT

OLIVIA'S WORDS echoed in Axel's head, even after he drove her back to her apartment and then sat beside her on the couch.

*Because you'll be there.*

But what if he wasn't? What if something happened that separated them? There could never be another replay of today's events. It could have ended so much differently, and he couldn't stomach the thought of that.

Plus, he couldn't deny that his feelings had started to grow for Olivia. That wasn't supposed to happen. It hadn't been his plan.

But when he had kissed her this evening . . . that had changed everything.

As he stared at her now, her face looking so earnest as she stared up at him, he felt his resolve melting. The resolve he'd held to not get close to anyone again. To remain at a safe distance from any potential romantic relationships in his life.

Maybe, in a way, flirting had been easy. There were no strings attached. No commitments.

But now he was actually feeling something...

Axel reached over and gently pushed a strand of her hair behind her ear. It was dark in the apartment, but he didn't have to have a lamp on to know that she was absolutely gorgeous.

His eyes went to her lips. Her full lips.

He'd already experienced what they felt like against his. Now he desperately wanted a replay.

Even though everything inside him told him to keep his distance, he knew the fight was futile.

The question was, did Olivia return his feelings?

As Olivia leaned closer, Axel's hand moved behind her neck. He nudged her face toward his.

Their lips met. This time, it wasn't for show. This time no one was watching or forming any opinions.

Axel felt things exploding inside him that he hadn't felt in years. As their lips explored each other's, he forgot about all his problems for a moment. Forgot about this case. Forgot about his divorce.

All that mattered right now was Olivia. Sweet Olivia.

That hadn't been his first impression of her. No, his first impression was that she was all sass and spice. But after getting to know her, he'd uncovered somebody different.

As he pulled away from their kiss, their gazes locked. He saw something in her eyes that he was certain matched what was in his own gaze.

And, if this was the case, then they were both in trouble.

---

OLIVIA FELT HER HEAD SWIRLING.

This time, it wasn't because she'd been drugged.

This time it was because of Axel's kiss.

She'd had no idea someone could kiss like that.

That a simple act could consume her as it did.

But now she knew nobody else's kiss would ever compare to that one. Would never compare to the kiss that had swept her off her feet and transported her away from her problems.

As she glanced up at Axel, she wondered if she could truly trust him.

She wanted to trust his story. Hearing about his past had touched her. And she felt like he was being sincere.

Yet another part of her remained cautious.

Tristan had been charming and sweet at first also. But he had pulled the wool over her eyes, and she didn't want to risk that ever again. If she wasn't careful, she could develop some strong feelings for Axel.

And she still wasn't convinced that was a good idea.

No matter how handsome he was. No matter how protective. No matter how he looked at her.

She had to be smart here. She didn't want to be one of those girls who jumped from one bad relationship to another. Tristan had been a bad enough relationship to last a lifetime.

Axel let out a long breath. "Listen, I don't feel right leaving you here by yourself tonight."

She braced herself for where he was going with this.

"How would you feel if I slept on your couch?"

She nearly laughed at herself. Her couch. Of course.

"I can't guarantee how comfortable it is."

He shrugged. "I'm a Navy SEAL. I'm sure I've been through worse."

She had to admit that she would feel better also if he stayed with her. The thought of being by herself right now wasn't comforting. Too much had happened.

And with that thought, she rose. "Let me go find you some sheets and a blanket."

And as soon as she handed them over to him, she was going to go to bed with her door locked and temptation separated from her.

## CHAPTER THIRTY-NINE

FIRST THING IN THE MORNING, Rocco called Axel.

Axel had hardly slept all night. He'd been too determined to listen for any signs of trouble.

There had been none.

But Axel had talked to his team a couple of times after the party. They'd called to check on Olivia. Axel had also asked them to recount who had been present when Olivia disappeared.

Gabe clearly remembered seeing Tristan in the group of people gathered around Mitch.

But if Tristan wasn't behind what happened to Olivia, then who was?

He supposed he could rule out Mitch since he was having an allergic reaction.

Axel's next best guess would be Leo, who was supposedly in the bathroom during the incident.

"Turns out, the power outage was legit at The Crazy Chefette yesterday," Rocco said.

Axel leaned against the kitchen counter, his coffee forgotten for the moment. "Good to know."

"No fingerprints were left by whoever pushed Olivia into the freezer, according to my sources, and no one saw anything."

Axel wished he could say that was surprising, but it wasn't.

"Did you hear anything off-record about what Olivia was drugged with last night?"

"I haven't heard anything officially—or unofficially. But we did some research. We think it was probably a roofie. She was drinking some sweet tea. I served it to her myself."

The bad feeling in Axel's gut grew deeper. "So the question is: when did she leave it alone for someone to put something in it?"

"When she wakes up, you might want to ask her. In the meantime, be careful."

"Will do."

"Those missing women are still out there, and they still need our help."

"You're right. Every day these women are missing, their chances to be rescued diminish." Those reminders had never left Axel's mind. "Do you know if the FBI has any leads?"

"My impression is that they don't."

"Hopefully that will change soon. What's on the agenda for today?"

"The Oasis Group hasn't asked us for any help today. Apparently, they have an event planned that doesn't require anyone serving food to them. We're trying to come up with another way to listen in on them. We're still monitoring their computer, of course."

"What would you like me to do?"

"You need to keep an eye on Olivia. After what happened last night, it's clear she isn't safe."

The thought of keeping his eyes on Olivia held its appeal in more than one way.

But he had to be careful not to let his emotions affect his job. When he'd agreed to act as her make-believe fiancé, he had no intentions of falling for her.

But maybe falling for her was just what he needed.

---

OLIVIA AWOKE to the scent of coffee.

It had been a long time since she had awakened to that aroma. She'd lived by herself for the past eight years, and she'd never mastered those programmable pots.

But she liked the aroma that floated into her room now.

Axel must have fixed coffee.

Warmth spread through her when she remembered that he'd slept on her couch. When she realized that he was here now. When she replayed that kiss in her mind.

That fantastic, fantastic kiss.

Olivia made herself presentable before stepping from her room and wandering into the kitchen. Axel sat at the table drinking his coffee. Black, of course. But she'd known that from his time in the restaurant. Maybe Olivia had been paying more attention to the man than she'd thought.

"Good morning," he called as he looked over his shoulder at her.

"Good morning." She almost felt shy as she said the words. In her whole life she had never been called shy. No, she had been the one who got in trouble for talking in class almost every single day.

Before she could even grab some coffee, Axel rose and strode toward the coffeepot. "How do you take your coffee?"

"Two sugars and cream."

"I've got it. Why don't you sit down?"

Olivia wasn't used to being spoiled, but she did as he asked. It actually felt good to have somebody wait on her for a change.

A moment later, Axel set a steaming mug in front of her before sitting across from her at the table. "How did you sleep?"

She'd stayed up for a while and done a quick internet search on her computer. She'd found several stories about the women who'd gone missing. She'd seen their faces. Studied their names. Lifted up prayers for their safety.

Then exhaustion had hit and she'd fallen asleep—and she'd fallen hard.

"All things considered, I slept pretty well," Olivia said. "You?"

Axel shrugged, and she could read between the lines. He'd hardly slept at all.

"Any updates?"

"The guys are wondering if you left your sweet tea unattended last night."

She paused and thought it through. "I suppose I could have left it on the deck railing at some point. People were mingling out there. I can't pinpoint anyone who might've gotten near it though."

Axel nodded. "Okay."

"I'm sorry. I know you guys are ready to close this case and move on."

"For the sake of the women who have been abducted, yes. But none of this is your fault." He paused. "Listen, Olivia. I'm sorry I didn't tell you the whole truth."

She wanted to be upset with him, but she couldn't be. She understood that there were some things people needed to keep to themselves.

"It's okay," Olivia said. "We just need to find these women. I want to do whatever I can to help."

"About that—"

Before he could finish the statement, Olivia's phone rang. She glanced at the screen.

"It's Stan. What do you want me to do?"

"Answer it," Axel said. "And put it on speaker."

## CHAPTER FORTY

AXEL LEANED FORWARD SO he wouldn't miss a word of the conversation.

Olivia forced a perky voice as she said hello.

"Olivia." Stan sounded equally as jovial. "How are you feeling? I heard you left early last night because you weren't feeling well."

She frowned. "I wasn't. Maybe it was something I ate. I'm not sure, but I'm doing much better today."

"I am glad to hear that."

"It's nice of you to call to check on me."

"Well, I did have other reasons as well. We're actually having a luau on the beach today. I wondered if you might like to come."

Olivia glanced at Axel. Axel rolled his finger in the air to encourage her to keep talking.

"I hate to impose on all your outings."

"You're practically one of us. And you're much nicer to talk to than all the stuffy people that I work with. You can even bring that fiancé of yours if you'd like. Seems like a nice enough guy."

"I would have to ask him, of course. When does it start?"

"It's at three. I hope you can join us."

Olivia glanced at Axel again, but he said nothing. "Let me check my work schedule, and I'll get back with you."

"That sounds like a plan. I hope I'm not disappointed."

As she ended the call, Olivia stared at Axel, waiting for his reaction. "What should I do?"

"You can't go." His firm voice left no room for argument.

A knot formed between her eyes. "What do you mean? Isn't this what you've been waiting for? Another opportunity to get some insider information? We're getting closer. I can feel it. Besides, Stan told us about the new phase of the company. If we can find out more about this concierge service and what it offers—"

"It's too risky. Especially after what happened last night. We're just going to have to rely on that computer that Gabe got into to find any more information."

Olivia wasn't ready to give up yet. "But being around these guys is the best way to figure something out, don't you think?"

"Maybe in theory. But it's not worth your life. There's no way you should go to that luau."

"Even if you're with me?"

"Even if I'm with you. We shouldn't have brought you into this, period. If I hadn't found you last night when I did . . ." He felt his gaze darken.

She frowned. Axel clearly didn't have to finish that statement because they both knew how it ended.

If he hadn't found Olivia, she could have disappeared for a long time. Maybe forever.

It was time to pull her out of this operation and figure out another way to get the information they needed.

---

OLIVIA WAS SCHEDULED to go in to work for a little while today. She was tempted to call in sick, but she didn't want to put Lisa in a bind.

One of the guys from Blackout had found her car. Apparently, whoever put her in that freezer had taken the time to find her keys and drive the vehicle to a parking lot near the lighthouse. They'd checked it for prints but found none.

Her mind continued to race as she dried her hair. She didn't want to say no to that luau. However, she knew how Axel felt about it.

But he was just being overprotective.

And being overprotective was *not* the way to find the answers that they needed.

Whoever was behind this needed to be stopped. They needed to be in jail.

But, for now, she got dressed in some jeans and a T-shirt as she readied herself to head to work.

Axel stepped toward her when she exited her bedroom, something clearly on his mind. "I've been thinking, and what do you think about this? I'll give you a ride to pick up your car, and then I'll follow you to work and make sure you get there okay."

"It seems like a lot of trouble for you to go through."

He stepped closer, his eyes warm and sincere. "You're worth it."

Olivia actually felt herself blush. She hadn't blushed in years until she met Axel.

"If you insist then I know I won't be able to stop you."

"No, you won't be." He leaned closer and quickly planted a kiss on her lips.

Immediately, Olivia found herself melting into a puddle.

She chided herself for letting him have that effect on her.

Ten minutes later, they both pulled up to The Crazy Chefette.

After Olivia parked her car, Axel climbed off his

bike and wandered toward her. He casually stood in front of her, almost looking as if he didn't want to leave.

"I guess I'll see you later," he finally said, a new intimacy to his tone.

"I guess." But Olivia really wasn't sure if that was the case or not.

She didn't know exactly how to define what their relationship was right now. If she wasn't going to help Blackout find answers anymore, did they even need to keep up this charade?

She didn't have any of those answers.

Axel continued to linger in front of her, his hands stuffed into his jeans and his black T-shirt stretched across the muscles of his chest. He was quite the sight to behold.

As Olivia felt her throat tighten, she looked away.

Finally, Axel said, "I'm going to get back to the office and see what I can do. I need to figure out some answers here. How late are you working?"

"Until five." Her throat continued to tighten as she stared at him—at his lips, specifically—and remembered their kiss.

It was best if she forgot it.

Sure, this had been a fun charade. But that's all it was.

Even when this was over, Olivia didn't know what she was doing with her life. If she was staying here. She didn't even know if Axel was the type looking for a relationship or if he'd been burned so badly that he was now single for life.

*Don't entertain the idea of a future together. Whatever you do. Don't—for the sake of your heart.*

So why when she stared at Axel's lips did Olivia only want to kiss him?

Axel started to reach for her but dropped his arm back down to his side. "I'll come back here and meet you when your shift is over. I don't want to take any chances."

She appreciated the concern in Axel's voice. The protectiveness. The notion—and action—wasn't something that she took lightly.

Nor did it clear her confusion.

"That sounds good." But Olivia's voice sounded scratchier than she would have liked. Why was she letting this man have this effect on her?

That could only mean trouble.

Olivia tried to ignore how alive her skin felt as Axel's arm brushed hers as he walked her to the door. He made sure she was safely inside before heading back to his bike.

Now it was time for her to get to work.

Maybe waitressing would keep her mind off Axel—and the danger surrounding her.

# CHAPTER FORTY-ONE

AXEL TRIED NOT to smile as he strode through the parking lot.

His emotions battled inside him.

On one hand, he wanted to revel in the fact that he actually felt something for Olivia.

On the other hand, he wanted to run. To protect his heart the way he protected others.

He was about to climb on his bike when a feminine voice called his name.

When he looked up, his stomach dropped.

"Kiki... what are you doing here?" She was the last person Axel had expected to show up.

"You weren't returning my phone calls." She sashayed toward him in a leopard-print dress and strappy sandals. "So I had to find an alternate way to talk to you."

He shook his head. "You shouldn't have come here."

She paused in front of him and touched his shirt, pretending to iron out a wrinkle. "But we need to talk."

"I already gave you my answer."

Her eyes flashed. "But I haven't even told you my proposal."

---

OLIVIA PAUSED JUST inside the door as she realized she still had Axel's jacket. He'd let her wear it when they took his bike to pick up her car.

She stepped back outside, and that's when she saw him talking to a woman.

A beautiful woman with bluish-black hair.

Olivia stopped and ducked back around the corner.

Her lungs froze when she realized what she was doing.

She shouldn't be hiding. She *should* announce her presence.

Yet she couldn't seem to move.

"You're the only one I want." The woman stepped closer to Axel.

"I'm flattered, but my answer stands." Axel only stared at the woman, unmoving.

"I'm pretty sure I can make you reconsider." The woman practically purred as she spoke and continued to inch closer to him. "I can give you everything you want."

"Kiki..."

Kiki? The woman's name was Kiki?

"Just listen, Axel. You know we could make this work. Admit it."

Axel didn't say anything for a moment until he chuckled. "*You* need to admit that whatever you think you can talk me into, you can't."

"That's not the impression I got from you last time we were together."

Had those two been a couple? Were they still a couple?

"I'm going to make your dreams come true, Axel. Every single one of them."

Olivia swallowed hard.

Had she totally misread Axel?

Because she refused to repeat the same mistakes from her past . . . and she suddenly felt like that was exactly what she was doing.

## CHAPTER FORTY-TWO

"KIKI, I already gave you my answer," Axel said. "It's a firm no. I wish you hadn't come here."

"You can't blame a girl for trying."

He climbed on his bike and put on his helmet. "Sorry to cut this short, but I have things I need to do."

"Important things?" She raised a shoulder and leaned her head toward it in that beguiling way she was known for. "Manly things?"

"I can't tell you that. But they're things I think are important." He started and revved his engine a moment. "Take care."

He hoped he'd resolved that issue. He didn't want to get his friends involved with it or raise their suspicions. If she kept being pushy, that's exactly what was going to happen.

He gave her a wave before pulling away.

As he headed down the road, he felt his vision blur again.

Not now.

If only he could predict when the ailment would hit him. But there was no rhyme or reason to how it came and went.

He pulled off the road, knowing he couldn't take the chance of not seeing something properly. It would put other people in danger.

As he stopped between the street and the ditch running alongside it, he glanced around him.

That same car from earlier in the week appeared in front of him—at least, that's how it looked, best he could tell. The one that had pulled out and run him off the road.

He blinked again.

Yes, that car was definitely headed toward him.

He had to move.

Now.

---

OLIVIA COULDN'T GET her mind off the conversation she'd just witnessed.

Who was that woman? Was Axel the player she'd first thought him to be?

"Ma'am, I ordered a lemonade not tea."

Olivia looked at the woman she was serving and frowned.

She was right. Olivia was supposed to deliver a lemonade.

Then the woman's face came into view.

It was one of the women who'd been flirting with Axel a few days ago.

Olivia bit back a scowl at the memory.

"Sorry about that," Olivia said. "I'll be right back with your drink."

She came back a few minutes later with the correct beverage.

"Say, you haven't seen that cute Navy SEAL in here lately, have you?"

Olivia's gaze darkened. "Axel?"

The woman smiled. "He's the one. I keep hoping I might run into him."

"Sorry. I haven't seen him. Did he give you his phone number?"

The woman snorted. "I wish. I tried to get it from him, but he didn't take the hint. Nothing I love more than a good challenge."

Wasn't this the type of woman Olivia had always seen Axel with? Someone who saw him as a conquest?

Then she realized what the woman had said.

She'd wanted Axel's number, but he hadn't given it to her.

Maybe Olivia really had been wrong about him being a player.

But, if that was the case, then who was that woman he was just talking to?

And the other question on her mind was this: would she ever be able to trust a man again after Tristan?

# CHAPTER FORTY-THREE

AXEL WATCHED the car as it continued toward him.

He couldn't just sit here.

He rubbed a hand over his eyes.

If only his vision would clear.

He was going to have to make this work.

Otherwise, that car would smash into him.

Quicky, he pulled back on the road.

Except, instead of heading away from the car, he headed toward it.

He twisted the throttle and zoomed down the road.

The car straddled the center of the street, still headed straight toward him.

Thankfully, no one else was around right now.

Axel clenched his jaw.

This was not the way this was all going to go down.

Sweat popped across his brow as he stared at the car.

The windows were tinted. He couldn't see the driver. His hazy vision didn't help.

As a test, he went to the left.

The car approaching him mirrored his actions.

This wasn't going to be easy.

He gripped his throttle more tightly.

Only ten more feet and this oncoming vehicle would hit him.

If this plan didn't work . . . he would be a dead man.

At the last minute, the approaching car gunned it.

Axel didn't have much time. They were playing a deadly game of chicken, and the stakes could cost him everything.

Six feet.

Four feet.

At the last second, Axel veered to the right, pulling his handle hard to barely miss the car.

He held his breath.

But it worked.

The car zoomed past, close enough that Axel could feel the heat coming from the metal. Close enough that the momentum made the hair on his arms stand on end.

He glanced behind him in time to see the car hit the brakes before speeding away.

He eased up on the throttle and let out a long breath.

That had been close.

Too close.

Who had been driving that car? And why did that person want to kill him?

---

OLIVIA HAD mixed feelings as she worked her shift at The Crazy Chefette.

On one hand, when she thought about Axel, she nearly felt elated. That was *not* something she expected to feel. Especially not about Axel.

But on the other hand, she remembered the events of this week and felt a cold, hard stab of fear. Tristan was here. Women were missing. Olivia herself had been locked in the freezer and drugged at the party.

Things could have turned out much differently. The common denominator in the situation was Axel. If he hadn't found her each time he had, Olivia might not be here right now.

The thought left her feeling unbalanced.

"I was hoping I might run into you again," a deep voice said.

She looked up and saw that man she had met . . . was that just yesterday? She couldn't remember. So much had happened, everything was a blur.

But it was the nice man. The boring one. The one who seemed like he had a desk job and that hated the gym.

The kind of guy she should like.

The complete opposite of Axel.

"You came back," she said.

"I decided I might have to come back to this place every day while I'm here in town."

"Do you like the food that much?"

"Something like that." But the smile he gave her indicated that there was more to it than that.

That he might be coming back to see her.

She felt flattered.

But she was also supposed to be engaged to Axel.

And until she was told otherwise, that was something that she needed to remind herself of.

For that reason she waved her hand in the air—the one with the fake engagement ring on it.

"Well, there's really nothing not to love about this place." She tried to brush it off and not lead the man on.

But if she hadn't met Axel when she did, maybe this guy would be somebody on her radar.

When Axel was done with this case and they were done with this fake relationship, maybe Olivia would be ready to move on.

But that kiss he'd given her last night. That hadn't been part of the charade. She was sure of it. What if he was beginning to have feelings for her? Would that change things after this op was over?

So many questions floated through her head. So much confusion.

Olivia tried to focus on her job and took the man's order before returning to the back.

As she did, she glanced at the time.

She needed to call Stan back and give him an answer. To tell him she wasn't going to make it to the luau.

She nibbled on her bottom lip.

But what if *she* did make it? Olivia knew that Axel had told her not to go. But she also knew that going would be a great way to find some answers.

It was in the daytime, and it was a luau on the beach. She could be careful. Even if Axel wouldn't be there, that didn't mean Olivia couldn't gain some information. In fact, maybe not being around him was her best chance for finding out something new.

With her mind made up, Olivia pulled out her phone.

She was going to call Stan. Then she needed to talk to Lisa and see if she could get off work a couple of hours early today.

## CHAPTER FORTY-FOUR

OLIVIA FELT a rush of nerves sweep through her as she pulled up to the house where the Oasis board members were staying.

Since Lisa let her off a few hours early, she'd had just enough time to head home and change into some jean shorts, a tank top, and sandals for this party.

If she had to guess, the luau was on the beach by the house. This would be a simple in and out. She wouldn't make waves or do anything foolish. Nor would she drink anything. Especially after what had happened last night. In fact, she'd stashed away her own bottle of water in her purse.

Guilt pounded her as she made her way toward the front door. Axel would not approve. But she needed to do this.

She brushed off her shorts one more time before walking up the steps. But before she even rang the bell, it opened.

Tristan stood there. He grinned when he saw her.

"I was hoping you might come." He glanced behind her. "Where is your fiancé?"

He said that last word as if it were a bad one.

"Couldn't make it, unfortunately."

"That's too bad." Tristan's words lacked any semblance of sincerity. "Everyone's out back at the beach. I'll walk with you."

Instead of going through the house, they headed down the stairs and toward the beach. A group of five people had gathered there wearing sunglasses, Hawaiian tops, and bathing suits.

Olivia was surprised she didn't see any grills or chairs set up to make the beach look more festive.

"Am I early?"

Tristan glanced at her, and a knot formed between his eyes. "What? No. Why would you ask that?"

"It just doesn't seem like the party is quite started yet."

He let out a chuckle. "That's because the party isn't taking place here. Didn't my dad tell you?"

"Tell me what?"

"We're getting on that boat, and they're taking us to a private island just off the shore. I thought you knew."

Her forehead tightened. No, she'd had no idea. She wouldn't have come if she knew she had to go to a private island for this event.

Panic rush through her. She should have told Axel. Somebody needed to know where she was going.

But before she could reach for her phone, Tristan took her arm and led her toward the water.

"Come on. We should get on this boat. It will be another thirty minutes until another one comes. This is going to be a fun time."

Somehow, she doubted that.

---

AXEL DECIDED to get to the restaurant a little early. Actually an hour and a half early. He'd grab a bite to eat and maybe catch up with Olivia a little bit as she finished her shift. He'd been thinking about her all day.

That was something he never thought he would say again. He hadn't been taken with somebody since Mandy. Look how that turned out. But Olivia seemed different than Mandy. More trustworthy. Like the kind of woman he could take at her word.

As he stepped inside The Crazy Chefette, he glanced around. But he didn't spot Olivia. She must be in the back.

He waited a few minutes until Lisa came out and then he strode over toward her. "Hey, Lisa. Where's Olivia?"

Lisa set her tray down on the breakfast counter and tilted her head. "I thought she was with you."

Axel's back muscles tightened. "What do you mean? Is that what she said?"

"She asked if she could get off a few hours early because she wanted to go to some type of luau. I just assumed you were going with her."

The air left his lungs.

Olivia had decided to go anyway? He hadn't seen that one coming. He thought they'd decided it was better if she didn't go—that it was too dangerous if she did.

Axel stepped back toward the door. "Thanks for the info."

Lisa knotted her eyebrows together. "Is everything okay?"

Instead of answering, he rushed out the door. He needed to get to the house where the Oasis crew was staying.

Because after what he had just heard, there was no way Olivia should be around these guys.

Mostly because a new threat had popped up on that computer.

One that said they had a new target they were going after today.

*They.*

That meant more than one person was in on this.

# CHAPTER FORTY-FIVE

WITH EVERY SECOND that passed as the boat sped away from the shore—away from Lantern Beach—Olivia felt a knot of anxiety growing in her stomach.

This was a very bad idea. Very bad.

Since they'd boarded the boat, Tristan hadn't left her side. He was being a little too attentive.

There were four other people onboard besides the captain. The only thing that brought Olivia any comfort was the gentle spray of ocean water and the sun as it hit her shoulders. The captain had gifted her with a pink lei as she'd boarded, but the fabric flowers felt scratchy against her skin.

At the moment, she sat at the back of the boat, one hand on the railing. She turned away from Tristan, who sat beside her, and tried to pretend like he wasn't there.

Apparently, Stan was already on the island. But Olivia had to wonder if that was true at all. This whole thing felt like one big trap.

"Why do you look so tense?" Tristan asked.

"It's just boats. Small boats on the ocean. Not my favorite." It wasn't a lie. They did make her nervous.

"In a moment, we'll go through the inlet to one of the smaller barrier islands between here and Cape Lookout. It'll be fine."

She nodded, even though she didn't feel like anything would be fine.

"Are you happy with that guy?"

Tristan's question startled her. That wasn't what she had expected him to ask. "Axel? Of course. I wouldn't have gotten engaged to him if I wasn't."

"But you were also engaged to me and you weren't that happy, were you?"

She scooted farther away from him, not liking where this conversation was going. "That was different, and you know it."

She didn't want to rehash these details with Tristan. But she had a feeling he was going to go there. She found comfort in knowing other people were around.

"Olivia . . . you've got to know that I cared about you." His voice cracked as if he were trying to be earnest. She didn't believe anything that came out of his mouth, though.

She refused to cower at his presence, even if there was a small part of her that wanted to flee right now.

"I cared about you too." She turned her head toward him but didn't look away from the water. She didn't want to give him the satisfaction of eye contact. "Until I saw your true colors."

"Ouch. But I guess I deserved that."

"Listen, no offense, but I don't want to talk about us. I'm only here because your father invited me."

"Is that the only reason you're here?" An ominous warning stained his voice.

She knew what he was getting at.

The secret he was holding over her.

Maybe she should just let him tell everyone.

She was so tired of his games.

"Of course, your father's invitation is the only reason I'm here," she told him. "Why else would I come?"

"I just didn't realize that you and my father were that close."

She felt the heat rising up her neck. "You know that your father likes me. You said so yourself."

"But I'm just not sure what *you're* hoping to get out of this outing."

Olivia felt the pressure beginning to crush her. Tristan wasn't giving up. "What I'm getting out of this is a luau. Who wouldn't want one of those?"

Just as she said the words, a strip of land appeared in the distance.

It looked like they were almost there.

And not a minute too soon.

But Tristan wouldn't back off . . . not until he got what he wanted.

Olivia had to figure out exactly how she was going to handle that.

---

AXEL PULLED up to the house rented by Oasis, quickly parked his motorcycle, and rushed toward the front door. He ran straight up the steps and knocked, but no one answered.

Strange.

But they were probably all outside.

He rushed around back to the beach and scanned all the faces there.

But no one from Oasis was out here either.

Where had they gone? Olivia hadn't mentioned that the luau was taking place anywhere else.

Axel grabbed his phone and called Rocco. Rocco agreed to call Bart and see if he knew anything.

Pacing the beach, Axel waited for a return call. Whatever was going on, he didn't like it.

"Well, look who's here."

He looked up and saw Mac MacArthur, the former

police chief on the island. The two of them had a few run-ins when Axel had been a teen, but the man, who was now the mayor, had become something of a father figure to him.

"You're not exactly dressed for the beach," Mac said.

Axel glanced down at his jeans, boots, and black T-shirt. No, he most certainly was not dressed for the beach.

"I was just looking for somebody."

"You mean the people on the boat that just took off from here?"

Axel's spine tightened. "What do you mean?"

He nodded toward the ocean. "I saw a bunch of people take off in a boat a little while ago. I overheard them saying something about a luau, which makes sense since they all wore leis around their necks."

"How long ago did the boat leave?"

Mac shrugged. "Probably twenty minutes ago."

"You didn't hear where they were going, did you?"

"No, but I assumed it wasn't very far away. I did hear somebody say that they were going to be back this evening."

"That was really helpful. Thank you, Mac. Let's catch up again soon."

Axel hurried toward his motorcycle.

He had to find Olivia.

Now.

## CHAPTER FORTY-SIX

A LOVELY SPREAD had been catered for the Oasis group on the island.

Olivia could see why the Blackout servers weren't needed here. The caterer himself had arranged all the food on the table, and everybody helped themselves to the picnic.

A volleyball net had been set up on the beach. A water trampoline floated just offshore. Music played. And a bonfire had even been started.

But Olivia wanted to be anywhere but here. She felt trapped. Her lungs felt tight. Her thoughts felt muddled.

Why had she done this? Why couldn't she have listened to Axel?

Just as on the boat, Tristan still hadn't left her side

since they'd arrived. He'd gone with her to get food, to walk the shore, to mingle with others.

Maybe she needed to use this as an opportunity to find out more information.

"It seems like Oasis is doing really well," she started before taking a sip of her water.

Tristan shrugged. "It is. I just need to get my foot in the door with my father."

She turned and scanned everyone around her. "Out of the everyone here, who's the most hands on?"

He narrowed his eyes. "Interesting question."

"I'm just making conversation."

Tristan let out a breath. "Not exactly what I want to talk about but . . . I don't really know. Mitch is over operations."

Mitch could be ruled out because he'd been having an allergic reaction last night when someone drugged her and carried her downstairs. She needed to dig deeper.

"Is Mitch the only one here who works that area?"

"He has a whole team under him. Why?"

"Anyone who's here?"

Tristan's eyes narrowed even more. "What are you getting at, Olivia?"

"Can't a girl just be curious?"

"I know a way to make people very curious about you . . ."

Heat rose on her cheeks. She knew exactly what he was getting at.

Olivia glanced up and saw Leo walking toward them. She knew things were probably about to get even more tense.

"Don't you look nice." Leo looked Olivia up and down without apology.

"Leave her alone," Tristan growled, his muscles bristling.

"I don't think I asked you."

"Since you always make poor decisions, I feel like I always need to insert my opinion." Tristan glared at his brother.

"I make poor decisions?" Leo laughed. "That's like the pot calling the kettle black."

A headache pounded between Olivia's ears. This was the last thing she wanted to listen to.

"I think I'm going to go grab some pineapple," she said. "You guys have fun with this conversation."

She wandered away before she had to listen to anything else.

What she really needed was to figure out who the bad guy was and then take herself out of this situation.

ROCCO WAS able to secure one of the boats at the Blackout facility and shuttle Axel to the island where the luau was taking place.

Rocco had called his contact, who told them where this island was. Apparently, he hadn't known about it in advance. It had been a last-minute idea.

Axel's thoughts continued to go to the worst places, however.

He hoped Olivia was okay. He hoped that he got there in time.

But there were no guarantees.

She should have never gone without him. What if she disappeared like those other women?

Axel couldn't let his mind go that direction.

Rocco slowed as they got closer to the island. On the other side, they could barely make out some people who seem to be having a party there.

Rocco pulled out of sight as he idled closer to the shoreline.

He secured the boat at a small dock and cut the motor.

Axel removed his boots and rolled his jeans before jumping out. He wished he'd had time to change. But he hadn't, so this was going to have to work.

"I'm going to stay over here just in case you need backup, but I'll try to stay out of sight," Rocco said. "As far as anybody else knows, you came by yourself."

"Good idea," Axel said. "I appreciate your help."

"The rest of the guys are on standby if we need them."

Axel hoped that it didn't come to that. But it very well could.

He tried to make his footsteps look casual as he sauntered down the shoreline. He would round the bend, where he should run into the Oasis party.

Then he needed to put on the show of his life.

He hoped that Olivia would follow suit.

As the crowd came into view, he scanned everyone there.

His heart skipped a beat when he saw Olivia in her jean shorts and a white tank top. She wore a lei and held a bottle of water in her hands.

Although relieved to see she was okay, his agitation returned to the surface.

She never should have come here alone.

Axel drew in a deep breath before releasing it.

Then he started toward her.

He prayed that this went okay and that no one got hurt.

## CHAPTER FORTY-SEVEN

OLIVIA LOOKED over her shoulder as she heard someone approaching.

Her eyes widened when she saw Axel walking toward her.

She quickly tried to hide her surprise.

"What are you doing here?" She tried to keep her voice light in case anybody was paying attention.

"I came to surprise you, of course."

As he said the words, Olivia glanced over and saw Tristan watching them.

Knowing she needed to put on a show, she closed the distance between them and threw her arms around Axel. "I'm so glad you were able to make it."

He held her close. "Me too. I am so glad my plans were able to change."

His voice hardened slightly with his words. He was

trying to send her a message. A message that coming here wasn't smart.

But Olivia already knew that. No one needed to tell her.

Axel stepped back and glanced around. "This looks like quite the party."

"It really is. You're going to love this barbecue."

She hated the stiff, wooden conversation. Especially when there were so many other more important things they needed to talk about.

But, for now, the two of them needed to continue to act the part.

Even though Olivia knew she was most likely going to get an earful from Axel later, she was relieved to see him. She already felt better knowing he was here.

She had a lot of questions for him.

"Why don't you show me around?" Axel's voice sounded sickly sweet.

She nodded and slipped her hand into the crook of his arm, determined to continue with their charade. "That sounds great. You can save your barbecue for later."

Only after they walked away from the crowd did Olivia feel like she could breathe. But she knew she'd left one battlefield for another. She braced herself for the oncoming conversation.

"What were you thinking?" Axel asked quietly as

soon as they were away from the crowds. The emotion was clear in his voice.

"I couldn't let this opportunity pass. I didn't know they were bringing me here and that it wasn't on the beach by the house."

"You should have never come to this island without me."

"Once I showed up at the house, I really had no choice but to carry through with it."

Axel glanced around, his eyes narrowing. "I don't like this."

"I don't either. But at least maybe I can find out some information."

Axel scanned the area again before pausing and stepping closer. "Olivia, there's something you need to know."

"What's that?" Olivia's heart pounded into her ears as she anticipated the bad news she felt coming.

"We were able to track a new message that went out this morning," Axel said. "These guys . . . they have a new target in their sights, and they plan on making a grab tonight."

Olivia shuddered at the thought. "I'm sorry to hear that."

Axel locked his gaze with hers. "I don't think you understand. We think that that next victim is . . . you."

AXEL WATCHED the fear wash over Olivia's face. Though he didn't want to see her looking scared, she needed to be scared right now. She should have never come here alone.

Her throat looked tight as she stepped closer and asked, "What now?"

"Right now, we have no choice but to play the part until we can make an easy getaway. We don't want to raise anybody's suspicions."

"I can't believe this. You really think I could be next?"

"Based on what happened last night, I definitely say yes. Besides, you fit the profile of the women they've been taking."

"But I thought these women were all abducted from hotels."

"That doesn't mean that's the only method they can use to secure their victims. In fact, I think you were supposed to be taken last night, but the plan was thwarted."

She shivered. "What do I do if they grab me?"

Axel felt the outrage grow inside him at the idea. He couldn't let that happen. "You're not going to be grabbed."

"But what if I am? What do I do then?"

He could barely stand the thought of it. He didn't want to answer. But Olivia was serious.

He swallowed hard. "If you're grabbed, stay low-key. Don't call attention to yourself. Don't be feisty. You just wait for us to find you."

"But you haven't found those other women yet. How would you guys find me?"

Axel frowned. She had a good point. But as much as he didn't like to think about this, there were no good solutions. The main point was that she shouldn't be grabbed.

He really didn't want to think about other possibilities. What he wanted was to keep Olivia safe. But eventually, he needed to deal with the reality that maybe that wouldn't be possible.

He pulled her into a hug, wrapping his arms tightly around her.

"Axel?" Her voice came out sounding soft and inquiring.

"I don't want anything to happen to you," he said.

"I don't want anything to happen to me either. But what if you guys planted a tracker on me? If I'm grabbed, I could lead you to the other women."

He backed away from her, all his muscles suddenly stiff. "That's a terrible idea."

"I think it sounds like it could be one of the best ones yet."

He shook his head. "*If* we had a tracker on you, and *if* you got taken, I wouldn't wait around to see where you ended up before coming after you. You have no training. You don't know what these guys might do to you. It's not happening. Understand?"

She raised her hands. "Okay, okay. I wasn't trying to get you upset. I was just trying to think of some solutions."

"We need to think of a different kind of solution. Okay?"

She nodded. "Okay. I understand."

Just the thought of Olivia being snatched made him realize just how much this woman had come to mean to him in such a short period of time.

Now Axel needed to figure out a way to keep her safe.

Always.

## CHAPTER FORTY-EIGHT

OLIVIA COULD HARDLY BREATHE. She couldn't believe that she had made that suggestion either, yet it seemed plausible. If those guys grabbed her, maybe she could lead everybody else to these other women.

But Axel was right.

Olivia had no training. Had no way to defend herself.

Plus, she couldn't fathom exactly what these guys might be doing. She almost didn't want to know.

She and Axel mingled among the guests at the party. Miranda hit on him again. Of course. Tristan tried to strike up what seemed like casual conversation, even though everybody knew it was anything but.

Olivia couldn't wait to get out of here. She wanted to hop on that boat Axel had brought over, return to her old life, and forget this had ever happened.

But what about those women? The ones who'd been abducted? They deserved justice.

They didn't have the opportunity to return to their regular lives and pretend like this was just a bad dream they could wake up from.

Olivia was in the position to help. The least she could do was to find out some information. But how could she do that without raising any eyebrows?

She didn't know.

She looked up as someone wandered up beside them. Stan.

He held a glass of whiskey—with a paper umbrella for show—in his hands and raised it in the air in greeting.

"Glad to see you could make it," he told Axel.

"Of course. Any time I can spend with Olivia is time well spent."

Stan chuckled. "I like that. Keep that attitude after you get married, and you'll be in for a long, happy life."

As they continued to chat, Miranda joined their conversation. As much as the woman annoyed Olivia, maybe she could use this moment to her advantage. As Miranda started asking Axel about his workout routine, Olivia took the opportunity to talk to Stan.

Olivia cleared her throat before bringing it up, praying that she could stay calm and not raise any red flags. "So I was watching the news this morning, and it said that a woman who was abducted from a hotel was found dead. That hotel is one of the ones your company services. What a frightening connection."

Stan frowned. "I know. We're doing everything we can to help the local and federal authorities figure out what is going on. We don't think it has anything to do with our chain of hotels in particular, but I suppose every possibility should be examined."

"It's scary." She rubbed her arm.

Stan's gaze met hers. "Yes, it is. Whatever's going on, I don't like it."

---

AS MIRANDA FLIRTED WITH HIM, Axel felt somebody else approach him on the other side.

Tristan.

"Can I have a moment of your time?" Tristan asked him.

Axel glanced at Olivia again. "I'm not letting her out of my sight, not after what happened last night."

"I can't blame you. We can have the conversation here. Miranda, would you excuse us?"

She stared a moment before nodding. "Of course."

As soon as she walked away, Tristan pulled out his phone and held it up. "Listen, you seem to like Olivia. I thought it would only be fair to give you a heads up about who she really is."

Axel's back muscles tightened. "Who she really is?"

What was he talking about?

Tristan showed him a picture on his phone.

Axel sucked down a breath as the image came into view.

It was a photo of Olivia lip-locked with . . . Leo.

Axel narrowed his eyes, feeling like this could be a trap. "What is that?"

Satisfaction gleamed in Tristan's gaze. "This happened while we were dating and when my brother was married. Olivia's not the innocent woman you think she is."

Axel tried to pull his gaze away from the photo, but he couldn't. The image was too startling, too repulsive. Olivia kissing a married man?

He shook his head, not wanting to fall into Tristan's trap. "I'm sure there's an explanation for that."

Tristan shrugged. "You can explain all you want, but this picture is undeniable."

"Yet she was the one who broke up with you." What sense did that make? There was clearly more to this story.

"This was the beginning of the end for us," Tristan said. "Olivia and I tried to make it work, but I couldn't get over her betrayal. She's calculated like that. She also wanted to steal Miranda's job. I just thought I'd warn you to be careful."

Axel swallowed hard, trying to push down his emotions.

He didn't want to believe that picture was real.

But it had *looked* real.

He knew firsthand that people could fake images like that. But he didn't think that Tristan was the type to do that. He didn't seem to have that skill set.

Plus, the man's claim might explain some of the tension he'd noticed between Olivia and Leo.

At once, Mandy's picture filled Axel's mind.

All the emotion from her betrayal flooded back to him.

Could Olivia be like Mandy? Was she the type who said she'd commit for life when in reality she was looking for the next conquest?

Axel glanced at her now as she was in a deep conversation with Stan.

He didn't want to believe it. But he knew he needed to keep his distance.

All those warm and fuzzy feelings he'd experienced would only end up getting him in trouble.

How could he have fallen for her story? How could Olivia have stayed with him even after he shared what he had last night?

He'd thought more highly of her.

But that had clearly been a mistake.

## CHAPTER FORTY-NINE

OLIVIA COULDN'T WAIT to get back to Axel and talk to him.

But, right now, she wasn't done with her conversation with Stan.

"I hope the police are able to figure out what's going on," she continued, thinking about the women who were missing and Stan's admission that it was scary.

"I've hired a private investigator to look into the matter," he admitted.

Olivia blinked. "You did?"

He nodded. "I need to know what's happening. That's the man who came to my door when you were over for dinner. I don't want any of my employees to know what's going on."

That made sense.

But if that was true . . . that definitely meant Stan wasn't a suspect.

As soon as she could, she wrapped up her small talk with Stan and made her way back toward Axel.

But, immediately, she noticed something had changed about Axel. He seemed colder, more distant. Why was that?

Panic pulsed through her veins. Olivia would like to think that Tristan wouldn't do something like that. But she knew she couldn't trust him. She wouldn't put anything past him.

"Is everything okay?" She studied Axel's face as she waited for his reaction.

His expression remained hard. "Look, I'm not one to play games. Tristan showed me a picture of you with Leo."

Olivia felt the blood drain from her face.

So he *had* done it.

Tristan had shared her secret.

And, now, Axel was wondering if he could trust her.

That was exactly what Tristan had wanted. He'd wanted to plant doubt in the mind of anybody who might have come to care about Olivia and ruin any chance of a relationship.

"It's not what you think," she started.

"I know what you're going to say. You're going to come up with some type of excuse."

"Axel, it really isn't what you think it is."

"Was the picture fabricated?" he asked.

Olivia nibbled on her bottom lip for a moment before shaking her head. "No. It wasn't."

"Then that's all I need to know."

---

"AXEL," Olivia called after him.

He'd started back to the party but changed his mind. Instead, he paused and stiffly turned toward her.

"Let me explain," Olivia rushed. "Please."

He remembered the excuses Mandy had given him. Axel *wanted* to believe Olivia was innocent. But could he?

He wasn't sure. He just needed a little space. But space was something he didn't have the luxury of right now. Not when so much was on the line.

He'd be lying if he said he wasn't disappointed in her.

But what if she was telling the truth? What if she really was the victim in all this? He didn't want to seem like he wasn't supporting her if that was the case.

He opened his mouth, about to tell her to go ahead.

Before he could, someone stepped next to them. "Excuse me."

Axel looked up and saw Cleveland standing there.

He looked nervous. Then again, the man always looked nervous.

"Could I talk to the two of you?" he asked. "It's important."

Axel's defenses rose. "What's going on?"

"I know who you are." Cleveland stepped closer and lowered his voice. "And I have the information that you need."

Axel glanced at Olivia.

Had this man discovered Axel was a part of Blackout?

Axel didn't know.

But he needed to hear this guy out.

Their safety could depend on it.

## CHAPTER FIFTY

OLIVIA FELT tension thread through her as they followed Cleveland away from the crowd.

How would Cleveland have found out anything?

Then again, the guy seemed detailed. Had he actually researched Axel's background? Because, if that was the case, there was a good chance he could have discovered Axel was a former Navy SEAL.

A sense of dread filled Olivia as she wondered what was about to play out.

She wanted the chance to explain the photo to Axel, but it looked like that wouldn't be happening any time soon.

When they reached the edge of the crowd, out of sight from everyone, Cleveland turned to them. "You are investigating Oasis, aren't you?"

Axel's gaze narrowed. "Why would you think that?"

"Listen, we don't have time for games," Cleveland rushed. "They're going to abduct another woman. Today."

Axel bristled. "Who's going to snatch another woman?"

"Leo and Tristan. I've been suspicious for a long time that they're involved in something illegal. But I overheard them talking earlier."

The blood drained from Olivia's face. Even though she'd figured that was the case all along, hearing the words leave Cleveland's lips only confirmed it.

"Why did you call us aside to tell us this information?" Axel's eyes remained narrowed as if he were suspicious.

Cleveland glanced back at the crowd in the distance. "Because I need your help before they enact their plan. I can't stay silent anymore."

Was this their chance to do something? To correct the wrongs that had been done?

"What can we do?" Olivia rushed.

Cleveland pushed his glasses up higher on his nose. "Maybe you can distract them."

"How do you propose we do that?" Axel asked. "And how will distracting them help anything?"

Cleveland frowned. "Because they're planning to abduct Olivia next."

His words hung in the air, offset only by the quickening pulse pounding in her ears.

Axel had been right. *She* was the next target.

Axel inched closer to her. "How do they plan on grabbing her?"

"Like this."

The next instant, something pressed into Olivia's side.

Something hard and small.

She gasped.

Something like... a gun.

Cleveland's face transformed from an uptight assistant into a cold-blooded killer. Through clenched teeth, he said, "If you make a move, I pull the trigger."

Olivia's heart pounded in her ears.

How were they going to get out of this one?

---

AXEL SAW the gun and sucked in a breath.

Although he was sure he could take Cleveland down, the gun added a whole new dimension to it.

He knew by the look in the man's eyes that Cleveland wouldn't be afraid to use his weapon. He wouldn't shoot Olivia. No, he wanted her alive.

Axel couldn't let that happen.

"Give me your gun," Cleveland said. "I know you have one on you."

Axel frowned as he pulled the gun from his holster.

"Set it on the ground. Don't try anything. I'll pull the trigger. Don't test me."

Slowly, Axel placed the gun on the ground. Instead of reaching down to pick it up, Cleveland nodded, indicating he should move forward.

"Now, start walking." Cleveland nudged the gun harder into Olivia until she let out a cry.

Axel raised his hands, trying to show that he wouldn't make any sudden moves.

Right now, the gun was too close to Olivia. It was too risky.

Axel did as Cleveland directed and began walking down the shoreline, farther away from the rest of the crowd. Rocco waited on the other side of the island. But what was the chance his teammate had seen any of this?

The island wasn't large, but trees obscured anything that was happening.

Axel needed to think quickly.

Just what was this man's plan? Where was he leading them?

When he saw the aluminum fishing boat in the distance, he got a better idea of what might be about to happen. They weren't staying on this island, were they?

"Why would you do this?" Olivia rushed, her voice sounding thinner than usual. "Why would you involve yourself in something like this?"

"Money. People use drugs once and they're gone.

But humans? They can be used over and over again. You fit the profile of who we're looking for. There's a whole class of men out there who don't want women grabbed from the streets. They want women who are classier. Smarter. Harder to break."

Axel's throat tightened as he swallowed.

"You don't want to do this." Olivia's voice cracked.

"But I do." Cleveland practically smirked as he said the words. "You got too close. You should have backed off."

"But..."

"Keep walking. Both of you. Enough talking. This isn't my first rodeo. Any sudden moves and someone will get hurt. I won't think twice about it."

Axel's mind continued to race. As soon as Cleveland pulled that gun away from Olivia for any reason, he would try to take the man down. But he couldn't take that risk right now.

"Were you the one who put me in the freezer?" Olivia asked. "And who drugged my water?"

"The freezer was just my way of trying to get you to back off. It didn't work. That's when we decided just to make you our next target. I slipped something into your drink. If we'd had five more minutes, you wouldn't be here on the island right now."

"You send your victims notes to make it look like they're being stalked—just in case anyone gets suspicious," Axel said. "Then you erase all the security camera footage, replacing it with generic video. You erase the keycard entry also, making it look like a ghost got in and out of these women's rooms."

Cleveland nodded. "And the technology allowed us to carefully pick out women who fit our profile. Smart, successful, single, without too many attachments. With this new platform we're about to launch, it will be even easier."

They reached the boat, and Axel paused. "What now?"

"Olivia and I are going to get inside."

Axel let out a breath. "You think I'm just going to stand here and watch that happen?"

Cleveland smiled.

The next instant, Cleveland's gun fired.

At Axel.

And pain spread across his chest.

## CHAPTER FIFTY-ONE

"AXEL!"

Olivia gasped as she saw him sink to the ground. She started to reach forward when Cleveland jerked her back.

"Not so fast," he growled.

She froze and looked up at him, her nostrils flaring with outrage—and fear. She couldn't deny the terror coursing through her now.

"You shot Axel! Let me help him!" She tugged against Cleveland's hold, desperate to tend to Axel.

"Leave him. You're going to get in that boat with me."

Olivia shook her head, knowing she would fight with everything in her before doing that. "You're crazy if you think I'm getting in that boat with you."

Something dark passed through his gaze. "We'll see about that."

The next instant, Olivia felt a prick.

She gasped and looked down at her arm.

Cleveland held a syringe.

He'd injected her with something.

Olivia tried to pull away.

But it was too late. Whatever had been in that needle was already coursing through her blood.

A moment later, everything faded around her.

When Olivia opened her eyes again, her arms and legs were bound. She was being lifted by someone from the small fishing boat into a larger boat.

Hazy images faded in and out.

But she still wasn't sure exactly what was happening.

She only knew she was powerless to stop anything.

When she came to the next time, she was lying on the floor in a dark room.

After a couple of seconds, she managed to pull her eyes open.

She sat up with a start, memories of what had happened hitting her at full force.

Axel had been shot.

She'd been abducted.

She grabbed her wrists. Her arms weren't bound. Neither were her feet.

But where was she now? Where was Axel? Was he still alive?

A cry caught in her throat at the thought.

Memories of the gun blast filled her thoughts. Memories of seeing Axel fall to the ground. Memories of Cleveland not allowing Olivia to help him.

What if Axel was...

She shook her head.

No. She couldn't think like that.

"It's okay," someone murmured beside her.

Olivia jerked her head toward the soft voice. As she did, her eyes slowly adjusted to the dimness.

A woman came into focus.

Lanie Smith.

One of the women who'd been abducted.

Just like Olivia.

She was with those other women.

A cry rose in her throat.

And she wasn't sure anybody was going to find them.

---

"AXEL?"

He pulled his eyes open and moaned as he felt the pain in his chest.

Rocco's face came into view. His friend hovered above him, concern stretched across his features.

"What happened?" Rocco helped him sit up.

Everything rushed back to Axel.

Olivia.

She was in trouble.

Pulling in a staggered breath, Axel dragged himself to his feet. The ache in his chest nearly took his breath away, but he ignored it.

"They took . . . Olivia," he muttered. "We've got to find her."

"We will." Rocco nodded at the tear in Axel's shirt. "But, first, were you shot?"

Axel raised the hem of his shirt, showing the black Kevlar there. "I wore a vest. Of course."

"Smart thinking," Rocco said. "All right, who took Olivia?"

"Cleveland. He's clearly working with somebody. He had a small aluminum boat he took her in. I'm guessing they transferred onto a larger boat that was waiting offshore."

Rocco's jaw tightened as he glanced at the open expanse of water beside them. "We've got to find her."

"I know. We've got to get the rest of the Blackout guys to help. There's no time to waste."

Rocco pulled out his phone. "I'll call the Coast Guard and the marine police as well. They can keep their eyes open."

Axel nodded, but he was afraid they might be too late.

He wasn't sure how long he'd been out. But it was long enough that the boat had disappeared from sight.

A bad feeling brewed in Axel's gut.

How could he have let this happen?

Now all he needed to concentrate on was making this right and finding Olivia.

## CHAPTER FIFTY-TWO

"WHERE ARE WE?" Olivia asked Lanie as she leaned against the wall and tried to clear her head.

"We're on some type of boat." Lanie continued to kneel beside her, a knot of concern between her eyebrows.

Olivia had introduced herself, and each of the women shared their own name.

None of them looked good.

One had a bruised eye. Their clothes were dirty. Their hair looked stringy and unkempt.

That wasn't to mention the fact that the room felt stuffy, musty almost. The odor of sweat lingered in the air, along with a sense of despair.

Olivia rubbed her forehead. This was a lot to take in.

"How long have you guys been down here?" she finally asked.

She knew how long ago they'd been abducted. Had they each been on the boat since then?

The four women in the room glanced at each other before shrugging.

"Two weeks."

"Six days."

"Ten days."

"I've lost count," the last woman said.

Olivia shuddered. "You're the women who went missing from the hotel rooms, right?"

Lanie nodded. "We drank the water that had been left in our rooms, and we all think that we were drugged."

"How did these people manage to get you out of your rooms?"

Lanie shrugged. "We don't know for sure. I suspect they put us in the laundry cart or an oversized piece of luggage. But everything is hazy."

Olivia glanced around, knowing she needed to do something to get out of this situation if she could. There was no time to waste.

"How many people are on this boat with us?" Olivia glanced at each of the women. "Does anyone know?"

"We've seen three men," Lanie said. "And they're all armed."

Despair tried to bite deeper.

Just then, the boat jostled, making Olivia's stomach jostle along with it. She hoped that now out of all times she did not get seasick.

She needed to be at her best right now if they were going to figure out something.

She stood and wobbled a moment before gaining her balance. Even though she knew the women here had probably already searched this room, Olivia needed to know what was here also.

There were no windows and just one door that she assumed was locked.

She walked closer, hoping to get a glance into the hallway from the small window over top it.

But before she could, the door opened.

Olivia blanched when she saw who stepped inside.

---

THE COAST GUARD, the marine police, and the local police were all out searching for Olivia.

Axel knew that should comfort him, but it didn't. He needed to find her. With every second that passed, he felt more pressure mount inside him.

The FBI had invaded the island. All the men from Oasis were officially being questioned.

Axel wished he could be in on the questioning, but he couldn't. There were too many other officials who had a place before him in line when it came to that.

But that didn't mean he was going to sit by idly either.

Axel and Rocco paced the shoreline now as they formulated their plan.

"Have we heard anything about any boats out on the water?" Axel asked.

Not yet," Rocco said. "The Coast Guard has questioned the occupants of any watercraft they've come across. But they don't have any answers yet."

Axel frowned, even though he wasn't surprised. "There has to be another way to find her. They have to be close. But as every moment passes, they could be getting farther and farther away."

"What are you suggesting?"

"I want to go out there," Axel said. "I want to search myself."

Rocco stared at him a moment before nodding. "The team goes in together. Understood?"

Axel nodded. "Understood."

He just hoped that everyone didn't take too long to get ready.

Because patience wasn't his strong suit right now.

Even with what he'd learned about Olivia, he knew he still cared about her.

He should have listened to her explanation.

Now he had to make things right.

# CHAPTER FIFTY-THREE

"YOU'RE... the guy from the restaurant." Olivia stared at the man who'd stepped into the room. Her bottom lip dropped.

The man smiled, an evil kind of smile that curled the sides of his lips but didn't reach his eyes. "That's me."

He was the one she'd thought looked like a desk jockey. The quiet, serious-looking man. The guy who was the total opposite of Axel.

Apparently, she'd underestimated who he was.

Because he was the one heading up everything, wasn't he? He had the perfect disposition to ensure no one got suspicious.

"I came to check on you and see how you're doing," he said.

She scowled up at him. "I'd be better if I wasn't in here."

"I can arrange for something like that."

A chill of fear swept through her. On second thought, maybe she was better off staying here.

"Who are you really?" she asked.

He scowled down at her. "My name is Richard Davis, and I'm the CEO of Good Day Stays."

She sucked in a breath. Another hotel chain. So maybe it wasn't an Oasis employee who was involved.

"So *that* was your connection. You made the guys from Oasis look like they were the ones behind this, but somehow you managed to hijack their system so they would look guilty instead of you."

"You're smarter than I thought you'd be. But, yes, you're correct. I managed to get Cleveland on board with me, and he showed me the ropes. We were able to access these women's rooms as well as security cameras without anybody knowing. It really worked out quite brilliantly. We could pinpoint the exact kind of women that my buyers are looking for."

Another stab of cold, hard fear shot through her. Olivia didn't even want to think about what the future might hold for her. She knew that she couldn't handle those facts right now. What she needed to concentrate on was getting out of here—and taking these women with her.

"What are you going to do with us?" The more Olivia knew, the more she could develop a plan.

"We now have all the women we need right now. We'll be heading down to an island in the Caribbean. It'll take a few days to get there, so you should just enjoy your trip. And don't worry. We'll be sure to pamper you as soon as we arrive. You'll have pedicures. Massages. Facials. Your hair will look nice and pretty."

Two women let out a cry behind her.

Olivia might have done so herself. She wasn't sure why she felt the need to be the protector of this group, but she did—even if she had no self-defense skills.

Certainly, she could think of *something* to do here. Creativity was her strength, after all. They all couldn't just sit back and wait for this fate to play out—a fate that had been assigned to them by evil men.

Olivia started to say something else when Richard grabbed her throat and pushed her back against the wall. "I said from the start that you were going to be trouble. That you weren't like the rest of them. I'm here to tell you that if you try to do anything, we'll make you pay. We won't kill you. But you'll wish you were dead."

Based on the look in his eyes, he was telling the truth.

But there was no way Olivia could accept what he had planned for her.

Absolutely no way.

"WHERE SHOULD WE GO?" Rocco asked over the roar of the motor.

It was getting dark, which only made this mission more complicated. But it didn't matter. Axel needed to be out here looking for Olivia.

The FBI and the rest of the agents could do their job on land. He'd heard they were taking a chopper out to search as well.

But he needed to be out here. On the water. This was what he was trained to do. Water rescues. Invasions. This was his specialty, along with the rest of his team.

They had taken two boats and had split up, even though they were communicating via phone.

"If my calculations are correct, at this point they could be up to three hours away," Rocco said. "That means that it will be nearly impossible to catch up with them, depending on what kind of boat they're in."

"When I watched the weather this morning, it showed a system developing in the Atlantic," Axel said. "I'm going to assume these guys aren't going north because of that. That means they'll head south and hope to stay out of the storm's path."

"That doesn't sound good."

"No, but it makes more sense to think they'd head

out into the ocean instead of the Pamlico," Axel said. "There are fewer places to hide in the Sound."

"So they're probably heading down the coastline."

Axel rubbed his jaw. "Have you called into all the ports to have them be on the lookout?"

"Cassidy said that she was going to do that."

"We need to put ourselves in the mindset of these guys," Axel said. "Where would you go if you had abducted these women?"

"It seems pretty clear that they're probably going to be used in some type of human trafficking ring. They could really go anywhere." Rocco paused. "But based on some intel I heard, it seems like the newest hot spot is a little known island in the Caribbean where the wealthy like to have extravagant parties."

"I've heard of that place, and you're right. That probably is where they are headed."

"So we need to figure out what this all means."

"It means we need to head out to sea also," Axel said.

Rocco didn't say anything a moment until finally nodding. "Let's do it. If we're able to spot something, that will give us an idea of which direction we need to go."

"That's right," Axel said. "We just need to pay attention. If we're smart, maybe we'll be able to track them down."

He prayed that was what would happen.

## CHAPTER FIFTY-FOUR

"ARE YOU OKAY?" Lanie sat down beside Olivia. Olivia nodded, even though she didn't feel okay.

After Richard put his hands around her throat, he'd smacked her across the face to drive his point home. Olivia's cheek still stung.

Then he'd pushed her to the floor and left.

What a nightmare.

Olivia wanted to think that this wasn't happening, but it clearly was.

Olivia glanced at Lanie. "We can't just sit here."

"We've all tried to think of ways to get out of this, but we've come up with nothing. And then the last woman to try to escape . . ." Lanie's voice trailed off.

Olivia studied her somber expression. "She died?"

Lanie nodded. "She tried to jump into the water to get away. She'd said she would rather take her chances in the ocean. But these guys went after her and made an example out of her for the rest of us. Cindy disappeared also, and no one knows what happened to her . . ."

Olivia shuddered. In some ways it didn't surprise her. But the fact did put more fear into her. Still, they couldn't give up hope. There had to be another way to figure this out.

The boat rocked again, and Olivia felt like she might get sick.

As she glanced around the dark room and the women there, she realized she didn't have any good ideas of how to escape. There was nothing here that she could use as a weapon. There wasn't even a pillow or a blanket.

The lei around her neck had been removed and her sandals were useless.

If they were going to get out of here, she was going to need some type of supernatural help.

---

USING BINOCULARS, Axel continued to search the horizon for any sign of life. But it was getting darker and harder by the moment. Plus the waves were getting bigger.

Still, he wasn't going to give up.

He desperately wished he could go back and listen

to Olivia's explanation. But he knew that that wasn't possible. They'd have to save that conversation for after Olivia was rescued.

"We're about halfway on our tank of gas," Rocco said. "What do you think we should do?"

Axel didn't have to think about it long. They couldn't turn back now. "I think we should go farther."

Before they could talk more, his phone rang. It was Colton.

"Just to let you know, we got a couple of radar images," Colton said. "It looks like you're heading in the right direction, but these guys are still a good hour ahead of you. That storm is coming in faster than we thought. I know this isn't what you want, but you should get back."

"Is the Coast Guard headed that way?" Rocco asked.

"They are, but they're in a bigger boat than you guys are."

"Understood," Rocco said.

But there was no way Axel wanted to go back now. Not when they were so close.

He just hoped the rest of the team agreed with him.

## CHAPTER FIFTY-FIVE

OLIVIA PULLED herself to her feet. She'd rather die than to go through with whatever plan these guys had orchestrated for them.

She knew that Axel said she should just remain low-key. But that wasn't going to happen. She wasn't called to be a coward. She was called to make a stand. To fight for the voiceless. The defenseless.

She certainly had more energy than the rest of the women here who'd been locked up much longer than she had.

Olivia stood and searched her pocket.

She pulled out a bobby pin she used to keep her hair back at the restaurant.

Her heart thudded in her chest. This might be just what she needed.

Bobby pins always seemed to work in the movies when it came to picking locks.

Would it work in real life?

It seemed worth a try.

She grasped the metal pin tight in her hands and knelt in front of the door.

"What are you doing?" Lanie asked.

"I'm trying to unlock the door."

"And then what?"

"I don't know. But I've got to find a way to stop this boat."

"It's like we said," Lanie reminded her. "There are three guys out there. There's no way you can take all of them."

"I know. That's why I'm going to have to use my brain instead of my muscles."

"I think this is a bad idea," another woman said.

"Does anybody have any other ideas?" Olivia asked.

No one said anything.

"This is what I'm going to do," Olivia continued. "I don't expect any of you to come with me. But I can't just stay here. I can't just accept that we are going to go to the Caribbean and be sold to the highest bidder."

She glanced back and saw all the women staring at her. But, still, no one said anything.

Finally, she turned back to the door and continued to work the lock.

She twisted the bobby pin, hoping it would catch

the right elements in the handle. She waited to hear the click that she was waiting for.

Finally, the lock clicked.

Olivia's breath caught.

Part of her really hadn't expected this to work. But she'd succeeded.

She stuck the bobby pin back into her pocket and turned to the women in the room. "I'm going to do everything in my power to find help."

Lanie's eyes were wide as she stared at her. "Olivia . . . be careful out there."

She nodded. "I will be."

Slowly, Olivia opened the door and glanced up and down the narrow hallway.

She saw no one.

She closed the door behind her so no one would have any indication she'd gotten out.

Then she slowly crept down the hallway.

She paused beside an emergency kit on the wall. Could there be something inside that might help her?

Olivia started to reach for it when she heard voices.

Quickly, she ducked into the closet behind her.

*Please, Lord. Don't let them find me. Please. These women need my help.*

She closed her eyes and waited for the voices to pass.

"I think this new one will be perfect for Zeke," someone muttered. "She's just his type."

"I've been telling him for a long time he needed to get in this kind of business. It's profitable. It will give him some cash flow until he gets what he wants."

Finally, the voices faded. Olivia waited another moment just to be sure.

But she heard nothing else.

Had they been talking about her? Who was Zeke? Exactly what were these men planning?

It didn't matter.

Whatever was going on, Olivia didn't like the sound of it.

Finally, she opened the door and crept out again.

Except this time she had a plan.

She went to the emergency kit she'd seen and pulled out a flare gun.

If Axel was out there, he needed to be able to locate them.

This was the best way to let him know about their presence.

Olivia only hoped—and prayed—that this worked.

---

AT LEAST AXEL knew they were going in the right direction. That realization brought him a small measure of comfort.

But he needed something more.

He needed a signal about where Olivia was.

Most likely, if she was on a boat, the captain had cut the lights. These people wouldn't want to be seen.

Rocco's and Axel's boat rocked back and forth with the waves and a misty rain had begun to fall on them.

His team had been in worse conditions—like that time in the Mediterranean Sea outside of Syria when rebel combatants had been out for blood.

They'd survived that.

Barely.

But they could survive this too.

"If we don't get back soon, we're going to run out of fuel," Rocco yelled over the sound of the waves and the motor.

Axel stared at the ocean around them. "We can't go back. Not yet."

"The most I can give you is thirty more minutes," Rocco said. "Otherwise, the storm will be on us and we'll be out of gas. We'll literally be dead in the water out here."

Axel frowned. He didn't like the sound of that.

He didn't want to put the rest of his team in danger. Beckett and Gabe were in the other boat, searching a different area of the ocean.

But they had a duty to find these women. With every minute that passed, those chances greatly decreased.

They continued to head out into the ocean, searching the area around them.

Twenty minutes later, the team still had nothing.

The first trickle of hopelessness tried to creep in.

Just as it did, Axel spotted something in the distance.

"Was that a flare?"

Rocco seemed to see it at the same time he did. He pointed to it.

"Do you think . . . ?" Rocco asked.

"I think that it's our best shot. We've got to go that way. Now."

# CHAPTER FIFTY-SIX

AS SOON AS Olivia shot the flare into the air, she tossed the gun into the water and ducked around the corner.

Those men would come to find her soon.

She had to make this as hard as possible.

But as she started around the side of the boat, footsteps sounded in front of her.

She couldn't go that way.

Instead, she swirled around and ran in the opposite direction.

She froze as she reached the bow of the boat. Misty water sprayed her skin as she glanced around.

She had nowhere to go, did she?

She couldn't risk jumping in the ocean.

With the waves looking as they did, that would mean certain death.

Her gaze stopped on a lifeboat that was secured against the cabin.

Moving quickly, she stashed herself behind it and waited.

Just in time.

Footsteps sounded across the deck.

"What just happened?" a deep voice asked.

"It sounded like somebody let off a flare."

"Who would have done that? The girls are locked up."

"Go check on them. Now. I'll look around and see if I can find anything."

Olivia pressed her eyes closed.

She didn't want to think about what that man would do when he found her.

Because he *would* find her.

There weren't that many places here on the boat to hide.

*Please, Lord, be with me. Be with those women. Protect us. Please.*

Olivia prayed that Axel had seen that flare.

If he was too far away, he'd never get here in time.

As lightning flashed in the distance, she realized a storm was headed this way. Just as the thought entered her mind, the boat lurched back and forth, and a faint layer of rain sprayed down.

Just how far offshore were they?

Olivia didn't know. She wasn't even sure how much

time had passed. Maybe it was better if she didn't know.

More footsteps sounded.

It was that same man.

He was coming to look for her.

Would he think to look behind this boat?

Eventually, she knew that he would.

Even if she was able to get away from him for the time being, where would she go?

She should have probably thought about that before she'd done what she did. But what other choice did she have?

The footsteps faded.

Had he gone away?

Should Olivia try to run back into the room and pretend like she had never left?

It was an idea. Maybe it was even worth considering.

Even if she would be trapped again.

She couldn't take on three armed men on her own.

Just as she peered around the boat to see if the coast was clear, she looked up.

The guard stood there with a gun pointed at her head.

AXEL AND ROCCO had the boat in sight. They'd already called the Coast Guard, as well as Beckett and Gabe, who were headed this way also.

So backup was on the way.

That was good news at least.

By Axel's estimation, his team should be able to approach that boat and board it without anyone knowing they were there. The overwhelming darkness would work to their advantage.

Axel's team had done operations like this a million times before. They'd come prepared.

Now, they just need to ensure their plan went through without a hitch.

However, they didn't know how many people were on that boat.

"Are you ready for this?" Rocco asked as he gripped the steering wheel.

Axel nodded, ignoring the spray of the ocean as another wave rocked the boat. Conditions were getting worse by the minute. But Olivia was all he could think about.

"As ready as I'll ever be," he muttered.

Rocco glanced at his phone and nodded. "The other boat is almost here. Let's go."

Wasting no more time, they puttered to the back of the yacht.

It wasn't an ideal situation, but nothing about this mission was ideal.

Just as they'd planned, Axel climbed aboard the stern of the boat. As soon as he stepped onto the deck, voices rang out.

He paused.

Was that Olivia? Was she the one who had set off that flare?

Axel wouldn't put it past her. She had that fire in her eyes. Even though Axel had told her if she was ever abducted that she should stay low-key, he hadn't for a moment thought she'd actually do that.

The voices floated through the air again.

That was *definitely* Olivia's voice.

"What were you thinking?" a man asked.

"I don't know what you're talking about." Her voice wavered.

Axel crept forward enough to see a man grasping Olivia's arm as he leered in front of her. Olivia tried to pull away, but the man wouldn't let her.

"Don't be smart with me," the man growled.

The man swung his hand across Olivia's cheek.

She gasped.

Anger flared to life inside Axel.

"I'm going to take you below deck and make you regret this," the man continued.

More anger surged through Axel's blood.

He didn't want to know what that meant. He needed to get to Olivia.

Now.

Raising his gun, Axel aimed it at the man. He had the perfect vantage point from here.

The next instant, he pulled the trigger.

The bullet pierced the man's shoulder.

As the man fell to the deck, Olivia gasped again.

The man raised his head, pain lacing his gaze. Despite his injured state, he reached for his gun again. His gaze swept behind him, no doubt searching for the shooter.

Searching for Axel.

Axel was *not* going to get shot again. His chest still throbbed from the first bullet he'd encountered today.

He rushed forward and pressed his foot down on the man's injured shoulder.

The man let out a cry of pain and released the gun.

As he did, Axel scooped up the weapon and shoved it in his waistband.

He pulled some zip ties from his pocket and tied the man's hands behind him.

One man down.

Axel didn't know how many more to go.

He glanced at Olivia as a light from the side of the cabin lit her face. "Are you okay?"

He blanched when he saw her black eye and the blood coming from her lip.

"You're alive . . ." Her voice cracked as she stared at him, relief filling her gaze.

"I'm alive. Are you okay?" He repeated the words

slowly. He had to know the answer. He had to know those men hadn't broken her.

Olivia seemed to snap out of her stupor and nodded. "Yes . . . yes. I'm fine."

Axel wanted to ask her more questions. To pull her into his arms.

But this wasn't the time.

Instead, he hoped his gaze conveyed just how happy he was to see her. "How many guys are on board?"

"Three. Two now if you don't include him." She nodded toward the man he'd just taken down.

Two? That was manageable. "How many women?"

"Four. They're below deck in a room at the end of the hallway."

"Rocco is headed down there now to get them." He leaned closer. "I need to help him."

"Of course."

As Axel led her toward the back of the boat so she could board the smaller watercraft, he heard a footstep beside him.

Followed by a gun being cocked.

## CHAPTER FIFTY-SEVEN

OLIVIA GASPED and scooted behind Axel as she turned and saw the man there.

Richard.

She had no idea how this was about to play out, but she didn't like the idea of anyone being hurt. Especially Axel.

Axel . . . who was alive and had come for her.

Hot tears flooded her eyes at the thought.

She'd thought she'd lost him.

Praise God she hadn't.

But this wasn't over yet.

"Put your gun down." Richard sneered as he said the words.

Axel didn't let go of his weapon. "You're the one who's going to put your gun down."

Richard scowled. "If you don't, I'll put a bullet in your girlfriend."

Axel stared at him another moment before slowly lowering his gun to the floor. He then raised his hands.

"How many people came with you?"

"There's just one other man on my boat," Axel said.

The man snarled. "You shouldn't have come here."

"You should never have taken those women."

"It's a little bit too late for you to have a say in that. You're just going to become another casualty in all this. You think that we can't take you down? Just because you're a former SEAL that you can take us all on?"

Olivia waited to hear what Axel would say.

When he didn't respond, she held her breath, praying for the best.

"You should have stayed away," Richard growled.

Then a bullet blasted through the air.

---

AXEL SAW blood spread across the man's shoulder just before he dropped to the deck.

As he did, Rocco appeared behind him and shoved his gun back into his holster. "Are you two okay?"

"We're fine," Axel rushed. "You?"

"We're clear here. We took care of the third guy, and Beckett and Gabe are with the women right now."

As he said the words, lights appeared in the distance.

The Coast Guard. They'd arrived.

Finally.

Axel's shoulders seemed to relax.

He turned to Olivia and pulled her into a hug.

"I'm so glad that you're all right," he murmured. "I'm sorry I let that man get you."

"You didn't let him get me. There was nothing you could have done." As her fingers touched his shirt, she felt the frayed fabric there. She pulled back to examine the bullet hole.

She sucked in a breath. It looked like it had hit him in the heart. So how . . . ?

"Bulletproof vest," he explained.

"You're . . . brilliant."

He winked. "I try."

Olivia clung tighter to him. Axel never wanted to let go.

As the Coast Guard approached, he let himself relax.

Maybe this whole nightmare could finally be over.

But just as that thought entered his mind, Beckett staggered onto the deck.

He was holding his shoulder.

Axel's breath caught.

Had he been shot?

# CHAPTER FIFTY-EIGHT

THREE HOURS LATER, all the women had been safely rescued and taken to the closest hospital to be checked out.

The FBI had arrested all of the men involved—including Cleveland who'd tried to catch a plane from a neighboring island so he could escape.

Olivia had been taken to the Lantern Beach Medical Clinic to be examined, along with Beckett.

Apparently, his shoulder injury had just been a flesh wound. *Praise God.*

Despite the odds, everything had turned out well in the end.

Once the doctor had deemed Olivia okay and released her, she quickly got dressed into some clean clothes Lisa had brought for her. Then she hurried out into the hallway.

She couldn't wait to talk to Axel.

Hopefully, to explain herself.

As soon as she stepped from her room, Olivia spotted Axel waiting at the door. He looked tired—but handsome. Sometime in the middle of this, he'd changed into a clean T-shirt and jeans. His hands were casually draped in his pockets. But his eyes were full of worry.

He instantly pulled her into a hug. Neither of them said anything. Their embrace felt like enough.

After a few minutes, Olivia looked up at him. There were still questions needing answers—important questions.

"How's Beckett?" she asked.

Axel didn't loosen his hold on her. "As ornery as ever. But he's fine."

"I'm glad to hear that." Her nerves kicked in as she looked up at him. There were things she needed to tell him—things that wouldn't allow her any peace until she spoke them aloud. "Axel, I want to explain that photo—"

"Olivia, I'm sorry I doubted you. I should have listened instead of jumping to conclusions."

"That's exactly what Tristan wanted to happen. He wanted to turn us against each other."

"And it worked—right when you needed me the most. I'm really sorry."

Olivia nodded. "I know what it looks like. But Leo

confronted me in his office. He planted that kiss on me and had a camera set up to record it. He wanted to hold it as leverage over me. Or Tristan. Or Stan. I'm still not sure what exactly he wanted to do with it. But I was not a willing participant in that exchange."

Axel stared at her as he waited for her to continue.

"At first, Tristan was mad at me and didn't believe me. Then he tried to use the photo to manipulate and control me."

"I'm sorry that he did that, but knowing what I do about him . . . I'm not surprised."

"I shouldn't be either." She glanced up at him. "Any other updates?"

Axel shook his head. "We haven't been able to determine yet who tried to run me off the road or who set off that bomb when Rocco and I were running. No one has admitted to it."

"Wait—you were run off the road? There was a bomb?" Why was this the first she was hearing about this?

He shrugged. "I didn't want to scare you. But I don't want to keep anything from you anymore either."

Her mind continued to race.

"Do you think those things could be separate incidents from everything else?"

He shrugged again. "We're looking into it."

Something about his gaze indicated there was more to that story. But what?

Olivia would save those questions for another day.

Axel started to lean toward her, his gaze softening. "Olivia..."

She swallowed hard as her eyes went to his lips.

She'd love more than anything to feel them against hers again. She wanted to smell his aftershave. Feel his muscles beneath her fingers.

As they stepped closer to each other, a commotion sounded around the corner.

Not a commotion.

Olivia glanced back and saw the rest of the Blackout team appear.

She and Axel stepped away from each other. They'd have to finish that at another time.

Instead, everyone chatted for a few minutes.

As a striking woman with deep red hair wearing a lab coat walked past, Gabe's gaze followed her.

"Nice coat," he muttered.

She looked over her shoulder and offered a soft smile. "Thank you." She kept her gaze on Gabe until she disappeared into another room.

"Nice coat?" Beckett grinned. "Good one."

"I had to think of something to say. Who is she? Does anyone know?" Gabe didn't bother to hide the awe in his voice.

"She's the new doctor in town," Beckett said. "She treated my shoulder."

"She's the most beautiful woman I've ever laid eyes

on." Gabe's gaze remained on the room she'd entered. "I'm going to marry her one day."

The rest of the team burst into laughter.

Even No-Smile Beckett.

"Sorry, Junior," Rocco muttered. "I think she's out of your league."

"I'd say," Axel agreed.

"Someone just grinned for the first time in six months." Rocco shook his head, amusement dancing in his gaze. "It looks like I lost my bet, and I'm going to be doing some paperwork for all you guys."

Olivia had no idea what they were talking about. But it was good to see the team laughing and smiling. That almost hadn't been the case.

As the rest of the guys trailed off in a conversation and gave Gabe a good ribbing, Axel pulled Olivia away from them. The amusement left his gaze.

"You probably know this already, but the FBI wants to talk to you."

"I know. I have to go down to the police station and give my statement." Cassidy had already been in and reviewed things with her.

"How about if I take you?"

Olivia smiled. "I think that sounds perfect."

But as they stepped around the corner, the woman Olivia had seen Axel talking with earlier appeared.

"Axel... I heard what happened."

His gaze darkened. "Kiki . . . what are you doing here?"

Olivia sucked in a breath.

Who was this woman to Axel?

---

"KIKI, I TOLD YOU MY ANSWER," Axel said. "You shouldn't have come here."

Her gaze went to Olivia. "Who is this?"

Olivia tensed beside him.

"She's no one you need to know about," Axel said. "Now, we need to go."

"I have other people I could talk to, you know." Kiki's voice almost sounded threatening.

"Then do that. I don't want any part of this."

"Axel . . . what's going on?" Olivia glanced up at him with questions in her eyes.

Axel scowled again. "Olivia, this is Kiki Smith. She's a reporter with Jam TV News."

"Jam TV?"

Axel nodded. "They want to do a documentary on me and my time as a SEAL. They're working with a publisher who would also offer a book deal to go along with it."

"I see. I take it that's not what you want?"

"Too many SEALs seem to be in for the fame lately.

I don't want to be one of them. There are some things that are best left quiet. Our missions are one of them."

"What about Operation Grandiose?" Kiki asked.

"Especially that one." Axel put his hand on Olivia's back. "We need to go. I'm flattered that you thought of me. But my answer is firm."

"There are other guys who will step in and take this deal," Kiki said. "But we like you. You were made for TV."

"I'm sorry. But good luck with your project."

With that said, Axel led Olivia outside.

Maybe he'd finally gotten Kiki off his back.

And he knew his choice was the right one.

There were some things that didn't need to be sensationalized.

Operation Grandiose was one of them.

## CHAPTER FIFTY-NINE

OLIVIA GRIPPED Axel's hand as they stood outside of Peyton's Pastries, a new business that was opening in town. As they waited there on the boardwalk, the scent of chocolate floated out.

Olivia had never realized how heavenly the scent was before.

The rest of the Blackout crew also lingered nearby to show their support.

Rocco absolutely glowed as he stood beside his girlfriend, Peyton, as she prepared to cut the ribbon. Then opening day would be in full swing.

"They look happy, don't they?" Axel whispered in her ear.

"They sure do." Rocco and Peyton looked like the picture of contentment as they exchanged glances and laughs with each other.

A few minutes later, Peyton held an oversized pair of scissors in her hand. She turned to address the crowd.

"I want to thank all of you for your support. Without you, I wouldn't be able to do this today. I especially want to thank Rocco. He's been my rock throughout all of this." As Peyton looked up at him, her cheeks turned rosy.

Rocco winked at her as he stood close with his hands casually draped in his pockets.

"That said, here goes nothing." Peyton cut the ribbon. "Now, the first one hundred customers get free cupcakes! Come on inside."

As people flooded that way, Axel and Olivia stood back.

Olivia had actually helped with Peyton's marketing campaign for today. As a result, several reporters had come to cover the opening. They'd also set up a nice online campaign.

"Good job," Axel said.

"Me? This was all Peyton's doing."

"I know you helped her. I'm glad you're giving this place a real chance."

"I think it's going to do great," Olivia said. "And I've tasted her cupcakes. They're delicious."

"They are pretty good. I can't deny that."

Olivia had decided to make the island her permanent home and work as a marketing consultant. She'd already picked up jobs with some local vacation rental companies, The Crazy Chefette, and a new bookstore that was opening later this summer.

Things over the past few weeks had ended up okay after all.

Cleveland, as well as Richard Davis would be spending a long time behind bars. It had also come out that Cleveland was the one who'd tried to have Stan run over that day when Olivia had saved his life. He was a truly vile man.

It didn't look like either Tristan or Leo would be taking over the company. Instead, Mitch would. All his secret phone calls? He and his wife were adopting a child from China and didn't want to tell anyone until it was finalized. He'd ordered a shipment of candy and treats so the child would feel at home once she arrived in the States.

The women who'd been rescued were all doing fine. They'd need counseling and support to recover from what had happened. But at least they were safe now.

And Olivia... She had Axel.

The past few weeks with him had been some of the best of her life. He'd taught her to surf, taken her on romantic dates including motorcycle rides to watch the sun set over the Pamlico Sound, and opened up to her in so many ways.

Although women still had eyes for Axel and tried to flirt with him, he didn't reciprocate.

He had eyes only for Olivia.

Axel caught her staring at him. "What?"

"I was just thinking about how grateful I am."

He rested his hands at her waist. "Why are you grateful?"

"Many reasons . . . you being one of them."

"I'm grateful for you also." He grinned. "Who knew a fake engagement would turn into this?"

Her grin matched his. "What can I say? That's how it all went down . . ."

"That's my girl." Axel beamed as he leaned forward and slowly planted a kiss on Olivia's lips.

~~~

Thank you so much for reading Axel's story. If you enjoyed this book, please leave a review!

## COMING NEXT: BECKETT

# ALSO BY CHRISTY BARRITT:

# OTHER BOOKS IN THE LANTERN BEACH SERIES:

LANTERN BEACH MYSTERIES

**Hidden Currents**

*You can take the detective out of the investigation, but you can't take the investigator out of the detective.* A notorious gang puts a bounty on Detective Cady Matthews's head after she takes down their leader, leaving her no choice but to hide until she can testify at trial. But her temporary home across the country on a remote North Carolina island isn't as peaceful as she initially thinks. Living under the new identity of Cassidy Livingston, she struggles to keep her investigative skills tucked away, especially after a body washes ashore. When local police bungle the murder investigation, she can't resist stepping in. But Cassidy is supposed to be keeping a low profile. One wrong move could lead to both her discovery and her demise. Can she bring justice to the island . . . or will the hidden currents surrounding her pull her under for good?

**Flood Watch**

*The tide is high, and so is the danger on Lantern Beach.* Still in hiding after infiltrating a dangerous gang, Cassidy Livingston just has to make it a few more months before she can testify at trial and resume her old life. But trouble keeps finding her, and Cassidy is pulled into a local investigation after a man mysteriously disappears from the island she now calls home. A recurring nightmare from her time undercover only muddies things, as does a visit from the parents of her handsome ex-Navy SEAL neighbor. When a friend's life is threatened, Cassidy must make choices that put her on the verge of blowing her cover. With a flood watch on her emotions and her life in a tangle, will Cassidy find the truth? Or will her past finally drown her?

**Storm Surge**

*A storm is brewing hundreds of miles away, but its effects are devastating even from afar.* Laid-back, loose, and light: that's Cassidy Livingston's new motto. But when a makeshift boat with a bloody cloth inside washes ashore near her oceanfront home, her detective instincts shift into gear . . . again. Seeking clues isn't the only thing on her mind—romance is heating up with next-door neighbor and former Navy SEAL Ty Chambers as well. Her heart wants the love and stability she's longed for her entire life. But her hidden identity only leads to a tidal wave of turbulence. As more answers emerge about the boat, the danger around her rises, creating a treacherous swell that threatens to reveal her past. Can Cassidy mind her own business, or will the storm surge of violence and corruption that has washed ashore on Lantern Beach leave her life in wreckage?

**Dangerous Waters**

*Danger lurks on the horizon, leaving only two choices: find shelter or flee.* Cassidy Livingston's new identity has begun to feel as comfortable as her favorite sweater. She's been tucked away on Lantern Beach for weeks, waiting to testify against a deadly gang, and is settling in to a new life she wants to last forever. When she thinks she spots someone malevolent from her past, panic swells inside her. If an enemy has found her, Cassidy won't be the only one who's a target. Everyone she's come to love will also be at risk. Dangerous waters threaten to pull her into an overpowering chasm she may never escape. Can Cassidy survive what lies ahead? Or has the tide fatally turned against her?

**Perilous Riptide**

Just when the current seems safer, an unseen danger emerges and threatens to destroy everything. When Cassidy Livingston finds a journal hidden deep in the recesses of her ice cream truck, her curiosity kicks into high gear. Islanders suspect that Elsa, the journal's owner, didn't die accidentally. Her final entry indicates their suspicions might be correct and that what Elsa observed on her final night may have led to her demise. Against the advice of Ty Chambers, her former Navy SEAL boyfriend, Cassidy taps into her detective skills and hunts for answers. But her search only leads to a skeletal body and trouble for both of them. As helplessness threatens to drown her, Cassidy is desperate to turn back time. Can Cassidy find what she needs to navigate the perilous situation? Or will the riptide surrounding her threaten everyone and everything Cassidy loves?

**Deadly Undertow**

The current's fatal pull is powerful, but so is one detective's will to live. When someone from Cassidy Livingston's past shows up on Lantern Beach and warns her of impending peril, opposing currents collide, threatening to drag her under. Running would be easy. But leaving would break her heart. Cassidy must decipher between the truth and lies, between reality and deception. Even more importantly, she must decide whom to trust and whom to fear. Her life depends on it. As danger rises and answers surface, everything Cassidy thought she knew is tested. In order to survive, Cassidy must take drastic measures and end the battle against the ruthless gang DH-7 once and for all. But if her final mission fails, the consequences will be as deadly as the raging undertow.

## LANTERN BEACH ROMANTIC SUSPENSE

**Tides of Deception**

Change has come to Lantern Beach: a new police chief, a new season, and . . . a new romance? Austin Brooks has loved Skye Lavinia from the moment they met, but the walls she keeps around her seem impenetrable. Skye knows Austin is the best thing to ever happen to her. Yet she also knows that if he learns the truth about her past, he'd be a fool not to run. A chance encounter brings secrets bubbling to the surface, and danger soon follows. Are the life-threatening events plaguing them really accidents . . . or is someone trying to send a deadly message? With the tides on Lantern Beach come deception and lies. One question remains—who will be swept away as the water shifts? And will it bring the end for Austin and Skye, or merely the beginning?

**Shadow of Intrigue**

For her entire life, Lisa Garth has felt like a supporting character in the drama of life. The designation never bothered her—until now. Lantern Beach, where she's settled and runs a popular restaurant, has boarded up for the season. The slower pace leaves her with too much time alone. Braden Dillinger came to Lantern Beach to try to heal. The former Special Forces officer returned from battle with invisible scars and diminished hope. But his recovery is hampered by the fact that an unknown enemy is trying to kill him. From the moment Lisa and Braden meet, danger ignites around them, and both are drawn into a web of intrigue that turns their lives upside down. As shadows creep in, will Lisa and Braden be able to shine a light on the peril around them? Or will the encroaching darkness turn their worst nightmares into reality?

**Storm of Doubt**

A pastor who's lost faith in God. A romance writer who's lost faith in love. A faceless man with a deadly obsession. Nothing has felt right in Pastor Jack Wilson's world since his wife died two years ago. He hoped coming to Lantern Beach might help soothe the ragged edges of his soul. Instead, he feels more alone than ever. Novelist Juliette Grace came to the island to hide away. Though her professional life has never been better, her personal life has imploded. Her husband left her and a stalker's threats have grown more and more dangerous. When Jack saves Juliette from an attack, he sees the terror in her gaze and knows he must protect her. But when danger strikes again, will Jack be able to keep her safe? Or will the approaching storm prove too strong to withstand?

**Winds of Danger**

Wes O'Neill is perfectly content to hang with his friends and enjoy island life on Lantern Beach. Something begins to change inside him when Paige Henderson sweeps into his life. But the beautiful newcomer is hiding painful secrets beneath her cheerful facade. Police dispatcher Paige Henderson came to Lantern Beach riddled with guilt and uncertainties after the fallout of a bad relationship. When she meets Wes, she begins to open up to the possibility of love again. But there's something Wes isn't telling her—something that could change everything. As the winds shift, doubts seep into Paige's mind. Can Paige and Wes trust each other, even as the currents work against them? Or is trouble from the past too much to overcome?

**Rains of Remorse**

A stranger invades her home, leaving Rebecca Jarvis terrified. Above all, she must protect the baby growing inside her. Since her estranged husband died suspiciously six months earlier, Rebecca has been determined to depend on no one but herself. Her chivalrous new neighbor appears to be an answer to prayer. But who is Levi Stoneman really? Rebecca wants to believe he can help her, but she can't ignore her instincts. As danger closes in, both Rebecca and Levi must figure out whom they can trust. With Rebecca's baby coming soon, there's no time to waste. Can the truth prevail . . . or will remorse overpower the best of intentions?

**Torrents of Fear**

The woman lingering in the crowd can't be Allison . . . can she? Because Allison was pronounced dead six years ago. Musician Carter Denver knows only one person who's capable of helping him find answers: Sadie Thompson, his estranged best friend and someone who also knew Allison. He needs to know if he's losing his mind or if Allison could have survived her car accident. Could Allison really be alive? If so, why is she trying to harm Carter and Sadie? As the two try to find answers, can Sadie keep her feelings for Carter hidden? Could he ever care for her, or is the man of her dreams still in love with the woman now causing his nightmares?

## LANTERN BEACH PD

**On the Lookout**

When Cassidy Chambers accepted the job as police chief on Lantern Beach, she knew the island had its secrets. But a suspicious death with potentially far-reaching implications will test all her skills—and threaten to reveal her true identity. Cassidy enlists the help of her husband, former Navy SEAL Ty Chambers. As they dig for answers, both uncover parts of their pasts that are best left buried. Not everything is as it seems, and they must figure out if their John Doe is connected to the secretive group that has moved onto the island. As facts materialize, danger on the island grows. Can Cassidy and Ty discover the truth about the shadowy crimes in their cozy community? Or has darkness permanently invaded their beloved Lantern Beach?

**Attempt to Locate**

A fun girls' night out turns into a nightmare when armed robbers barge into the store where Cassidy and her friends are shopping. As the situation escalates and the men escape, a massive manhunt launches on Lantern Beach to apprehend the dangerous trio. In the midst of the chaos, a potential foe asks for Cassidy's help. He needs to find his sister who fled from the secretive Gilead's Cove community on the island. But the more Cassidy learns about the seemingly untouchable group, the more her unease grows. The pressure to solve both cases continues to mount. But as the gravity of the situation rises, so does the danger. Cassidy is determined to protect the island and break up the cult . . . but doing so might cost her everything.

**First Degree Murder**

Police Chief Cassidy Chambers longs for a break from the recent crimes plaguing Lantern Beach. She simply wants to enjoy her friends' upcoming wedding, to prepare for the busy tourist season about to slam the island, and to gather all the dirt she can on the suspicious community that's invaded the town. But trouble explodes on the island, sending residents—including Cassidy—into a squall of uneasiness. Cassidy may have more than one enemy plotting her demise, and the collateral damage seems unthinkable. As the temperature rises, so does the pressure to find answers. Someone is determined that Lantern Beach would be better off without their new police chief. And for Cassidy, one wrong move could mean certain death.

**Dead on Arrival**

With a highly charged local election consuming the community, Police Chief Cassidy Chambers braces herself for a challenging day of breaking up petty conflicts and tamping down high emotions. But when widespread food poisoning spreads among potential voters across the island, Cassidy smells something rotten in the air. As Cassidy examines every possibility to uncover what's going on, local enigma Anthony Gilead again comes on her radar. The man is running for mayor and his cult-like following is growing at an alarming rate. Cassidy feels certain he has a spy embedded in her inner circle. The problem is that her pool of suspects gets deeper every day. Can Cassidy get to the bottom of what's eating away at her peaceful island home? Will voters turn out despite the outbreak of illness plaguing their tranquil town? And the even bigger question: Has darkness come to stay on Lantern Beach?

**Plan of Action**

*A missing Navy SEAL. Danger at the boiling point. The ultimate showdown.* When Police Chief Cassidy Chambers' husband, Ty, disappears, her world is turned upside down. His truck is discovered with blood inside, crashed in a ditch on Lantern Beach, but he's nowhere to be found. As they launch a manhunt to find him, Cassidy discovers that someone on the island has a deadly obsession with Ty. Meanwhile, Gilead's Cove seems to be imploding. As danger heightens, federal law enforcement officials are called in. The cult's growing threat could lead to the pinnacle standoff of good versus evil. A clear plan of action is needed or the results will be devastating. Will Cassidy find Ty in time, or will she face a gut-wrenching loss? Will Anthony Gilead finally be unmasked for who he really is and be brought to justice? Hundreds of innocent lives are at stake . . . and not everyone will come out alive.

**LANTERN BEACH BLACKOUT**

**Dark Water**

Colton Locke can't forget the black op that went terribly wrong. Desperate for a new start, he moves to Lantern Beach, North Carolina, and forms Blackout, a private security firm. Despite his hero status, he can't erase the mistakes he's made. For the past year, Elise Oliver hasn't been able to shake the feeling that there's more to her husband's death than she was told. When she finds a hidden box of his personal possessions, more questions—and suspicions—arise. The only person she trusts to help her is her husband's best friend, Colton Locke. Someone wants Elise dead. Is it because she knows too much? Or is it to keep her from finding the truth? The Blackout team must uncover dark secrets hiding beneath seemingly still waters. But those very secrets might just tear the team apart.

**Safe Harbor**

Guilt over past mistakes haunts former Navy SEAL Dez Rodriguez. When he's asked to guard a pop star during a music festival on Lantern Beach, he's all set for what he hopes is a breezy assignment. Bree hasn't found fame to be nearly as fulfilling as she dreamed.

Instead, she's more like a carefully crafted character living out a pre-scripted story. When a stalker's threats become deadly, her life—and career—are turned upside down. From the start, Bree sees her temporary bodyguard as a player, and Dez sees Bree as a spoiled rich girl. But when they're thrown together in a fight for survival, both must learn to trust. Can Dez protect Bree—and his carefully guarded heart? Or will their safe harbor ultimately become their death trap?

**Ripple Effect**

Griff McIntyre never expected his ex-wife and three-year-old daughter to come to Lantern Beach. After an abduction attempt, they're desperate for safety. Now Griff's not letting either of them out of his sight. Bethany knows Griff is the only one who can protect them, despite the fact that he broke her heart. But she'll do anything to keep her daughter safe—even if it means playing nicely with a man she can't stand. As peril ripples through their lives, Griff and Bethany must work together to protect their daughter. But an unseen enemy wants something from them . . . and will stop at nothing to get it. When disaster strikes, can Griff keep his family safe? Or will past mistakes bring the ultimate failure?

**Rising Tide**

Benjamin James knows there's a traitor within his former command. The rest of his team might even think it's him. As danger closes in, he must clear himself and stop a deadly plot by a dangerous terrorist group. All CJ Compton wanted was a new start after her career ended under suspicion. Working as the house manager for private security group Blackout seems perfect. But there's more trouble here than what she left behind. As the tide rushes in, the stakes continue to rise. If the Blackout team fails, it's not just Lantern Beach at stake—it's the whole country. Can Benjamin and CJ overcome their differences and work together to find the truth?

# ABOUT THE AUTHOR

*USA Today* has called Christy Barritt's books "scary, funny, passionate, and quirky."

Christy writes both mystery and romantic suspense novels that are clean with underlying messages of faith. Her books have won the Daphne du Maurier Award for Excellence in Suspense and Mystery, have been twice nominated for the Romantic Times Reviewers' Choice Award, and have finaled for both a Carol Award and Foreword Magazine's Book of the Year.

She is married to her Prince Charming, a man who thinks she's hilarious—but only when she's not trying to be. Christy is a self-proclaimed klutz, an avid music lover who's known for spontaneously bursting into song, and a road trip aficionado.

When she's not working or spending time with her family, she enjoys singing, playing the guitar, and exploring small, unsuspecting towns where people have no idea how accident-prone she is.

Find Christy online at:
  **www.christybarritt.com**
  **www.facebook.com/christybarritt**
  **www.twitter.com/cbarritt**

Sign up for Christy's newsletter to get information on all of her latest releases here: **www.christybarritt.com/newsletter-sign-up/**

**If you enjoyed this book, please consider leaving a review.**